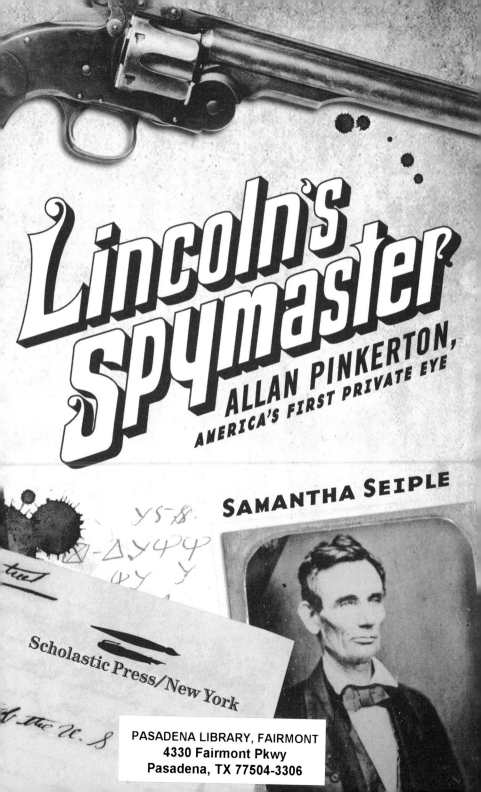

Lincoln's Spymaster

ALLAN PINKERTON, AMERICA'S FIRST PRIVATE EYE

SAMANTHA SEIPLE

Scholastic Press/New York

FOR TODD

CONTENTS

THE PLAYERS

The Pinkerton Detective Agency

Allan Pinkerton

Timothy Webster

Kate Warne

George Bangs

Harry Davies

Hattie Lawton

Pryce Lewis

John Scully

Sam Bridgeman

William "Billy" Pinkerton

Robert "Bob" Pinkerton

Joseph Whicher

Louis Lull

James McParland

The Union

President Abraham Lincoln

General George B. McClellan

Brigadier General Jacob Cox

Colonel Thomas A. Scott

General Ambrose Burnside

The Rogues' Gallery

The Reno Brothers Gang

Frank Reno

John Reno

Simeon Reno

William Reno

John Moore

Henry Jerrell

Frank Sparks

Grant Wilson

Albert Perkins

Miles Ogle

Charlie Anderson

Volney Elliot

Charlie Roseberry

Theodore Clifton

Michael Rogers

The James-Younger Gang

Jesse James

Frank James

Cole Younger

Jim Younger

John Younger

Bob Ford

The Confederacy

President Jefferson Davis

General Robert E. Lee

General Henry Wise

Rose Greenhow

Colonel George S. Patton

The Baltimore Plotters

Cypriano Ferrandini

Otis Hillard

James Luckett

Border Ruffians/Proslavery

William Quantrill

William "Bloody Bill"
   Anderson

Jesse James and associat

Barber Cypriano Ferrandini, a leader in the Baltimore Plot.

Prologue
Into the Conspirators' Nest

Baltimore, Maryland, February 15, 1861
17 days before Abraham Lincoln's presidential inauguration

"Never, never shall Lincoln be president," said Cypriano Ferrandini, his eyes burning with anger. "He must die—and die he shall."

Ferrandini glowered at the men sitting at the table with him in the corner of a dimly lit saloon. His body shook with fury as he continued to speak.

"With the first shot the chief traitor, Lincoln, will die, then all Maryland will be with us, and the South will be forever free."

The men hung on to his every word, spellbound. To outsiders, Ferrandini was just a barber from Italy. But to those in the know, the fiery and influential Ferrandini was the leader of the Palmetto Guards, a secret group of rebels who were ready to fight to the death.

"Murder of any kind is justifiable and right to save the rights of the Southern people."

When Ferrandini finished speaking, everyone at the table fiercely agreed with him. Cigar smoke swirled in the air, and the men were warmed by the whiskey and a feeling of camaraderie from being in complete agreement with one another. No one suspected there was a spy sitting at the table, ready and waiting to betray them.

The spy was Allan Pinkerton—a name known for striking terror and hatred into the hearts and minds of criminals.

But Ferrandini and the other men at the table knew him by the name John Hutchinson. And while Pinkerton sat at the table agreeing with them that Lincoln must die, he was fully aware of the fact that *they* were the real traitors. Nevertheless, Pinkerton also knew that if he made one false move or said one wrong thing, he would likely end up dead.

With the election of Abraham Lincoln three months ago, anger was raging over the issues of slavery—not just in Baltimore but across the nation. Bitter and savage debates caused the simmering rage to explode, and a person could find himself murdered over a difference of opinion.

Fearful that Lincoln would abolish slavery, the fight escalated, with six states seceding, or breaking away, from the United States and forming their own country. There was talk that rebel troops were getting ready to seize Washington, D.C., and overthrow the government as the United States and the newly formed Confederacy teetered on the brink of a civil war.

Abraham Lincoln's favorite portrait, which he
used for his presidential campaign ribbons.

For the past two and a half weeks, Pinkerton had been
working undercover, posing as a secessionist. He had set up
an office in Baltimore's financial district and befriended
James Luckett, who happened to work in the same building.

When they first met, Pinkerton told Luckett that he was
a stockbroker from Georgia, a state that had just seceded
from the United States. Luckett, in turn, told Pinkerton that
he was a secessionist and fully supported the Southern states'
right to own slaves. Luckett went on to tell him that he
believed Maryland should break free from the Union and
join the Confederacy. Strategically, Maryland's geographic
position was important since all the roads from the North
passed through it and into the South.

Pinkerton acted as if he wholeheartedly agreed with Luckett, and the two hit it off immediately. Over the course of the conversation, Pinkerton brought up Lincoln's impending presidential inauguration. Everyone was talking about it. In fact, four days ago, Lincoln had boarded the train in his hometown of Springfield, Illinois, to begin his journey to Washington, D.C.

Lincoln planned on making ninety-two stops along the way in Illinois, Indiana, Ohio, Pennsylvania, New York, New Jersey, and Maryland. He wanted to meet and greet his supporters before being sworn in as president. To make sure everyone knew about his trip, his train schedule was published in all the newspapers. Lincoln was expected to arrive in Baltimore on February 23, just eight days away.

"He may pass through quietly, but I doubt it," said Luckett.

Luckett confided to Pinkerton that there was a secret organization called the Palmetto Guards that was powerful enough to put a stop to Lincoln becoming president of the United States. Even though Luckett wasn't a member of the organization, he was friends with the leader, Cypriano Ferrandini, and he was helping the Palmetto Guards raise money so they could buy more guns and ammunition.

Luckett praised Ferrandini, saying he was "a true friend of the South" who was not only willing to die for the cause but who also had "a plan fixed to prevent Lincoln from passing through Baltimore."

Pinkerton listened carefully, calculating his next move. To gain Luckett's trust and show solidarity to the Southern cause, Pinkerton took out his wallet and gave him a twenty-five-dollar donation—a very generous amount of money for the time.

Pinkerton told Luckett that he "had had no doubt . . . that the money was necessary for the success of this patriotic cause."

The tactic worked.

Luckett offered to introduce Pinkerton to Ferrandini so he could meet the man who was going to put his generous donation to good use. Pinkerton didn't hesitate to accept the invitation, willing to take his chances and risk his life.

Now he found himself at the same table with Luckett and Ferrandini, trying to find out the details of the plan to assassinate Lincoln.

"But have all the plans been matured, and are there no fears of failure?" Pinkerton asked Ferrandini.

"Our plans are fully arranged and they cannot fail. We shall show the North that we fear them not," said Ferrandini.

"But about the authorities," Pinkerton asked. "Is there no danger to be apprehended from them?"

"Oh, no, they are all with us."

Ferrandini went on to assure him that soon "the North shall want another president, for Lincoln will be a corpse."

Before Pinkerton could find out any more, the meeting ended abruptly. Ferrandini suspected that two strangers sitting at a nearby table were eavesdropping. Worried that the strangers might be spies, Ferrandini decided to leave.

Pinkerton was anxious to secretly follow Ferrandini but he was asked to stay behind and keep an eye on the strangers. Ferrandini wanted to make sure that the two suspicious-looking men didn't follow him. Not wanting to look suspicious himself, Pinkerton agreed and told Ferrandini that if the strangers were spies, he would be sure to "whip them."

Not long after, Pinkerton returned to his hotel room. He sat down and wrote a report about his meeting with Ferrandini. Even though Pinkerton still didn't know how Ferrandini planned to assassinate Lincoln, there was one thing he knew for sure. He was about to embark on the most important mission of his career.

Allan Pinkerton, the most famous detective of the time, would have to find a way to save Abraham Lincoln's life.

Allan Pinkerton, America's first private eye.

Chapter 1
An Unsuspecting Detective

Dundee, Illinois, June 1846
Fifteen years earlier

It was a hot summer day when twenty-six-year-old Allan Pinkerton paddled his raft a few miles up the twisting Fox River. When he reached a small unnamed island, not far from the neighboring town of Algonquin, he splashed through the cold water, making sure to secure his raft so it wouldn't float away.

No one lived on the island. But Pinkerton had discovered that there was an abundance of trees, free for the taking. This was a real boon to his barrel-making business, where a hand-painted sign hung over the entrance of his cooperage that read, THE ONLY AND ORIGINAL COOPER OF DUNDEE.

Once he was ashore, Pinkerton scouted the island for trees to cut. As he made his way to the center of the island, where the underbrush was thick, he was surprised to find burning embers and ashes in a campfire.

To Pinkerton, it didn't take a genius to figure out what

was going on. No one had time to picnic, especially not here. Everyone was too busy working, trying to make ends meet. He easily deduced that somebody was up to no good.

"No honest men were in the habit of occupying the place," said Pinkerton. "As the country was then infested with coin counterfeiters and desperate horse thieves."

But whoever had made the campfire was no longer there. So Pinkerton set off to work, gathering his supplies. Once he loaded them on his raft, he made his way down the river, back to his cooperage.

Pinkerton had been the cooper in Dundee for three years now. Born and raised in the Gorbals, the toughest and poorest slum in Glasgow, Scotland, Pinkerton never planned on living in America—not until he broke the law and became a "wanted man."

"I had become an outlaw with a price on my head," said Pinkerton.

Pinkerton's trouble with the law began when he was twenty years old and joined the Chartists, a group of people who banded together trying to promote the rights of the working class. The Chartists wanted every man to have the right to vote and to improve working conditions, especially in the factories where workers had fifteen-hour workdays and weren't allowed to join trade unions or strike for better pay.

Pinkerton was a well-known and outspoken Chartist. At meetings he made fierce speeches, and his views were printed

The house in Scotland where Pinkerton was born and raised.

in newspapers. However, the Chartists weren't always peaceful at their demonstrations. They weren't afraid of violence or causing riots, and the police weren't afraid to use force against them.

"I wasn't on the side of the law then. . . . Wherever we showed our heads, the police clubbed us," said Pinkerton.

Pinkerton also participated in the "Newport Rising." Armed with old muskets, axes, sledgehammers, and iron bars, about four thousand Chartists marched to the town of Newport, Wales. When they arrived in the town square to demand the release of Chartist prisoners, they were met with a hailstorm of bullets fired from the authorities. Dozens died and many were injured. Pinkerton escaped.

"It was a bad day," Pinkerton said. "We returned to Glasgow by backstreets and the lanes, more like thieves than honest workingmen."

Queen Victoria and Parliament feared a revolution and considered Glasgow as "one of the places where treasonable practices prevailed to the greatest degree."

Treason or not, being poor was something Allan Pinkerton was all too familiar with. Allan, who was a serious and quiet child, lived in a run-down two-room tenement with his parents and older brother, Robert. When Allan was ten years old, their circumstances became even worse when his father died.

Pinkerton's mother, Isabella, worked at a mill, but there was never enough money or food. When his mother did have a little extra money, she would bring home an egg for them to eat—a rare and special treat.

Right after his father died, Pinkerton, who was an avid reader, had to drop out of school. He got a job as an errand boy, working, he said, "from dawn to dusk for pennies." After two years of what he called a "dreary existence," twelve-year-old Pinkerton decided to learn the trade of barrel making. He became a cooper when he was eighteen years old.

Two years later, the police were hunting him down for being a Chartist, determined to arrest him for treason. Pinkerton became a fugitive, fleeing the country. He and his new bride, Joan, were smuggled onto a ship that was heading for America.

It was a treacherous trip. The ship sank off the coast of Nova Scotia, Canada, and when they rowed their lifeboat to shore, they were robbed. Nearly penniless, there were a few things Pinkerton still had—determination, ambition, and a friend.

Taking quick action, Pinkerton contacted the local coopers' union, which helped him find work making barrels. Not long after, Pinkerton and Joan made their way to Chicago, where Pinkerton's friend, Robbie Fergus, a fellow Chartist who had also fled Scotland, greeted them warmly and offered them a place to stay. Fergus also helped Pinkerton find work making barrels for a brewery. It wasn't long before Pinkerton and Joan had saved enough money to move to the nearby frontier town of Dundee, Illinois.

Dundee, Illinois, suited Pinkerton. The town, with a population of nearly three hundred, had a few country stores, a post office, two blacksmith shops, a mill, and two taverns. Down the road, near the wooden bridge that crossed over the Fox River, was Pinkerton's very own home and cooper shop, which he built from the ground up.

Business was good. Pinkerton's barrels were well crafted and sold at a fair price. His reputation quickly grew for his honesty and strong work ethic. Soon he had eight apprentice coopers, some of them runaway slaves. An outspoken abolitionist, Pinkerton detested slavery.

Even though it was against the law to help runaway

Allan Pinkerton and his wife, Joan.

slaves, Pinkerton never hesitated to do whatever he could to help them. Illinois was a major route on the Underground Railroad, the secret network of escape routes for runaway slaves, and Pinkerton's home was a "station," or safe house. He and his wife, Joan, gave the runaway slaves food and shelter. Pinkerton also taught some of them carpentry and the cooper trade, so they would be skilled workers and have a chance to earn a better living.

"I have assisted in securing safety and freedom for the fugitive slave. No matter at what hour, under what circumstances, or at what cost, the act was to be performed," Pinkerton later wrote.

Although Pinkerton was willing to risk his life to help others, he was a cautious businessman, always pinching pennies. Pinkerton's thriftiness was what led him to discover the plentiful supply of wood on the uninhabited island up the Fox River.

The discovery of the campsite on the island weighed on Pinkerton's mind. He couldn't stop wondering about it, wanting to know what was going on there. Finally, he made a decision that was going to change the course of his life.

In the middle of night, under the cover of darkness, Pinkerton decided to go back to the island. Hiding in the tall marshy grass, he waited. And waited. And waited some more, until he suddenly heard oars splashing in the river. In the shadows he could see the outline of a boat rowing toward the island.

Pinkerton watched the men come ashore and make their way to the campsite. Then he waited and watched, carefully inching his way closer. Pinkerton could see them crowding around a blazing campfire. Although he couldn't hear what they were saying, Pinkerton could hear the clanking noise of metal. He quietly crept away.

The next morning, Pinkerton went to the town's sheriff. He told him what he'd witnessed, and then Pinkerton took the sheriff to the island so he could see it with his own eyes. The sheriff agreed—something suspicious was going on.

Soon after, in the dead of night, Pinkerton and the sheriff, along with his posse, raided the island.

"I led the officers who captured the entire gang," said Pinkerton.

They found large amounts of bogus coins and the tools that they used to make the counterfeit money. By morning, Pinkerton was the town's hero, and everyone was talking about how he helped capture the scheming "coneys." From that time on, the unnamed island on the Fox River was called "Bogus Island."

Pinkerton went back to the business of barrel making, believing that was the end of his crime fighting. But he quickly discovered it was just the beginning.

✕

Not long after Pinkerton helped nab the coneys on Bogus Island, the local sheriff made him his deputy. He helped the sheriff rid the area of more coneys and horse thieves. Word quickly spread to the crime-plagued city of Chicago, and in 1847, he was asked to join their police force.

Pinkerton soon learned firsthand that there wasn't much of a police force. The police officers weren't required to have any previous experience, and they didn't receive any formal training. They worked only at night, patrolling the city on foot and keeping a lookout for crimes and fires. They also had a bad reputation for shirking their duties and drinking on the job. As a result, the police force couldn't keep up with the widespread crime.

The *Chicago Tribune* newspaper advised its readers to take matters into their own hands.

Chicago's courthouse, where Pinkerton worked as a deputy sheriff and as the city's first-ever detective.

Our citizens cannot be too cautious about their dwellings and stores. Be prepared to greet midnight prowlers with a dose of cold lead, and they will quickly stop their operations.

To make matters worse, the police force was controlled by the local politicians. The mayor decided who was hired and fired. Corruption was widespread.

Allan Pinkerton was the exception. He made a lot of arrests and, at the same time, a lot of enemies. After two years on the job, in 1849, the mayor chose Pinkerton to be Chicago's first detective.

Driven by a strong sense of "bare-knuckle" justice, Pinkerton chased after criminals and never backed down— using his fists, if needed, to get the job done. Once Pinkerton zeroed in on a criminal, there was no stopping him; he was uncompromising.

"The detective should be hardy, tough, and capable of laboring unknown to those about him," he said. "I shall not give up the fight with criminals until the bitter end."

Pinkerton didn't like the political corruption in the police force. Even though he was promoted to detective, Pinkerton left after a year to open his own detective agency. It was a chance for him to call the shots and earn more money to support his growing family.

A strict father, Pinkerton and his sweet-natured wife were busy raising two sons, William and Robert, and a daughter, Joan, in a white clapboard home on Adams Street in Chicago. Their two-story home was within walking distance to Pinkerton's National Detective Agency.

Located on the corner of Washington and Dearborn Streets just one block from the courthouse and jail, Pinkerton's National Detective Agency was the first of its kind. Unlike the Chicago police force, Pinkerton was always open for business, working night and day. His detective agency's logo was a wide-open eye with the slogan "We never sleep," making him the only and original "private eye" of Chicago.

From the start, Pinkerton's detective agency was different from most police agencies. Pinkerton didn't believe in the idea that it takes a thief to catch a thief. He believed a detective should be honest.

"The profession of the Detective is a high and honorable calling . . . he is an officer of justice, and must himself be pure and above reproach," Pinkerton wrote. "The public have a right to expect this from their officers . . . they have a right to know that their lives and property are to be guarded by persons, male or female, of whose integrity there can be no question."

When Pinkerton hired new detectives, he looked for people who were adaptable, reliable, and honest. He didn't care if they had any previous experience, because he would train them. And he also didn't care if they were a man or woman.

Pinkerton raised eyebrows when he hired the first-ever woman detective, which was unheard of at the time, but that

Pinkerton's logo of an eye with the slogan "We Never Sleep" is credited with giving rise to the term private eye.

didn't concern him. He was more interested in her ability to investigate and obtain information in circumstances where a man couldn't.

Pinkerton, who was the first to call his detectives "operatives," pioneered the technique of going undercover—using a disguise and acting a part—so he could secretly infiltrate situations to gain access to the suspect of the crime without raising suspicion. He also perfected the art of shadowing, or following, a suspect without being detected.

"As a detective ... Mr. Pinkerton has no superior, and we doubt if he has any equal in this country," the *Chicago Democratic Press* reported.

A hard-nosed boss, Pinkerton expected all of his detectives to follow his code of ethics and be relentless in their pursuit of criminals. As a result, Pinkerton detectives, or "Pinks" as they were called, were known for being incorruptible, causing criminals to fear and hate them.

"I hated the Pinkertons as thoroughly as the corrupt police did because of their interference ... Nevertheless, I had to acknowledge that they were honest, and it was dangerous for a crook when a Pinkerton was on his trail," George White, a notorious safecracker, stated.

As Pinkerton's reputation grew, so did his business. In 1855, the rich and powerful railroad companies soon came knocking at his door. The new and rapidly expanding railroads were easy targets for crime, especially for thieves and vandals. Since the local police force didn't cross state lines, they weren't much help to the railroads.

To solve this problem, Pinkerton created his own private police force that worked across state lines to protect the railroads. One of the big problems the railroad companies had were their own employees stealing from them.

In 1860, Pinkerton made headlines in the newspapers for the capture and conviction of an Adams Express railroad employee who'd stolen $40,000, an enormous amount for the time. Pinkerton and his undercover detectives recovered nearly all of the embezzled money.

So when Pinkerton received a letter from Samuel Felton, the bespectacled president of the Philadelphia, Wilmington & Baltimore (PW&B) Railroad, on January 27, 1861, Pinkerton thought, at first, it was business as usual. He never suspected it would lead to uncovering a plot to murder Abraham Lincoln. Until he arrived in Baltimore.

General Principles of Pinkerton's National Detective Agency

◇ Never accept any reward money. A Pinkerton detective can't be bribed or bought.

◇ Never use a "stool pigeon." A Pinkerton detective doesn't pay criminals for information.

◇ Always write a detailed daily report. A Pinkerton detective keeps the client in the know and never overcharges them with unnecessary expenses.

◇ No cases involving divorce or marriage. They just lead to scandal.

◇ No testimony from drunk witnesses. They aren't credible.

◇ All suspicions must be verified by facts. Always be impartial and guard against prejudices. The goal of every investigation is the whole truth.

Chapter 2
A Murderous Plot

February 1, 1861
22 days before Lincoln's arrival in Baltimore

Allan Pinkerton was worried. He and his operatives had just arrived in Baltimore, and they were already under the gun.

Samuel Felton had hired Pinkerton to find out if rebels in Baltimore planned to destroy the railroad line. Reliable sources had secretly informed Felton that "there was an extensive and organized conspiracy throughout the South to seize upon Washington." The rebels planned to destroy the railroad lines so Northern troops couldn't be transported to Washington, D.C., "to wrest the capital from the hands of the insurgents." And once the rebels ruled the capital, Lincoln wouldn't be sworn in as president.

Felton was alarmed because his very own PW&B Railroad line was a vital link connecting the North to Washington, D.C. After he first heard the troubling news, Felton contacted the authorities in Washington and Baltimore. But neither were any help. So he turned to Pinkerton.

Samuel Felton, the president of the PW&B Railroad, hired Pinkerton to uncover the nest of conspirators in Baltimore.

Pinkerton told Felton that he and his team of operatives would find out if conspirators even existed and if they were really planning to destroy Felton's railroad line. If they did exist, Pinkerton and his team would infiltrate and shadow the suspects. He explained how they would "become acquainted with some of the members," and would "learn their secrets and proposed plans." To achieve any of this without raising suspicion, they would be undercover.

But befriending suspects took time—sometimes years. Pinkerton warned Felton that the biggest danger was the short amount of time they had to pull off the investigation— there were just a few weeks before Lincoln's train would

George Bangs (left), Pinkerton's right-hand man, with soldiers on the battlefield.

pass through Baltimore. So Pinkerton suggested doubling up on the number of operatives, so they could "attack on every point we can find accessible."

Pinkerton brought his best operatives for the mission. George Bangs, Pinkerton's sharp right-hand man, ran their headquarters, receiving reports and handing out Pinkerton's assignments. Bangs had been a New York City police officer before garnering headlines for Pinkerton's National Detective Agency when he tracked down and captured the famous French counterfeiter Jules Imbert.

Kate Warne, the first-ever woman detective, was assigned to live in Baltimore and pose as a rich Southern lady from Montgomery, Alabama, using the alias Mrs. Barley. She was to blend in, befriend prominent ladies in society, and find out anything about the conspiracy. As part of her disguise, Warne pinned a black-and-white cockade on her dress. This "badge," which was stamped with the image of a palmetto tree, signaled to other Southerners that she was a secessionist.

Pinkerton had no doubt that she was up for the task. A brilliant conversationalist and a good listener, Warne had been instrumental in helping Pinkerton recover the $40,000 for the Adams Express Company, and she had recently been promoted to manage Pinkerton's newly created Female Detective Department.

Pinkerton sent Timothy Webster to Perrymansville, Maryland, about thirty miles from Baltimore, where a rebel cavalry troop was armed and rigorously training. Webster, who was originally from England, had been a police officer with George Bangs in New York City. He was not only good with a gun but also a shrewd and daring spy.

"Fear was an element entirely unknown to him," said Pinkerton.

Webster's undercover assignment was to pose as a secessionist and join the rebels. Webster, who was usually quiet and reserved, transformed himself into the role. It took him only a few days before he was a member of the cavalry. He was partnered with Hattie Lawton, a new woman detective at the agency. They posed as a married couple.

Pinkerton also chose Harry Davies for the mission. Davies had originally studied to be a Jesuit priest before changing his mind and working for Pinkerton. The well-educated Davies spoke several languages and had traveled extensively throughout the world.

"He had a thorough knowledge of the South, its localities, prejudices, customs, and leading men, which had been derived from several years' residence in New Orleans and other Southern cities, and was gifted with the power of adaptation," said Pinkerton.

He assigned Davies the role of an extreme secessionist, and he was to live at the famous Barnum's City Hotel on the

Pinkerton's undercover agent and
Union spy, Timothy Webster.

corner of Calvert and Fayette Streets near the Battle Monument. Barnum's was considered the best hotel in the city of Baltimore and a hot spot for secessionists. It was also one of the most dangerous spots for a Union spy.

Like Davies, Pinkerton also hung out at Barnum's, where he eavesdropped and made conversation. Pinkerton and Davies were careful never to be seen together. They couldn't risk blowing their covers.

"There every night as I mingled among them, I could hear the most outrageous sentiments enunciated," said Pinkerton. "No man's life was safe in the hands of these men. . . . Those Bullies were all armed and would not hesitate on the slightest provocation to use these arms to shoot down a Union man."

On February 10, five days before Pinkerton met Ferrandini, he received a letter from a master mechanic of the railroad. The news was alarming.

"I am informed that a son of a distinguished citizen of Maryland said that he had taken an oath with others to assassinate Mr. Lincoln before he gets to Washington, and they may attempt to do it while he is passing over our road . . . This information is perfectly reliable."

The scope of Pinkerton's investigation suddenly widened from preventing the destruction of the railroad line to also saving Lincoln's life.

"I immediately set about the discovery of the existence of the conspiracy and the intention of its organization,"

Pinkerton wrote. He knew that "coolness, courage and skill could save the life of Mr. Lincoln, and prevent the revolution which would inevitably follow his violent death."

On February 16, the day after Pinkerton met Ferrandini, Pinkerton went to Barnum's, hoping to have a "chance" meeting with him. Pinkerton needed the detailed facts of Ferrandini's plan. But he and Ferrandini didn't cross paths. Pinkerton was worried that the mission was failing.

Until February 19, when Timothy Webster reported to Pinkerton that he'd learned firsthand the rebels definitely planned to cut the telegraph wires so news of Lincoln's death couldn't be reported. They also planned to burn the bridges and destroy the railroad tracks so Northern troops couldn't take the train to Baltimore.

Time was running out. Lincoln was due to arrive in Baltimore on February 23—just a few days away. With this information in hand, Pinkerton turned to his undercover operative Davies.

In the past several days, Davies had made friends with the hard-drinking Otis Hillard, a regular fixture at Barnum's. Hillard was an obvious choice to befriend because he discreetly wore a gold badge on his chest that was stamped with a palmetto, indicating that he was a secessionist. Davies had learned that Hillard was a member of the Palmetto Guards, the secret military organization Ferrandini was the leader of.

Davies reported to Pinkerton that while having dinner with Hillard in a private dining room, he tried to get

Barnum's City Hotel, where the Southern rebels met and the Pinkerton spies listened.

Hillard to talk about the Palmetto Guards. At times, it wasn't easy.

"We have taken a solemn oath, which is to obey the orders of our captain, without asking questions, and in no case, or under any circumstances reveal any orders received by us, or entrusted to us, or anything that is confidential," said Hillard.

Davies carefully pressed him for more information. He asked Hillard what their first objective was.

"It was first organized to prevent the passage of Lincoln with troops through Baltimore, but our plans are changed every day," said Hillard.

Although Davies tried, he also couldn't find out any details.

"I cannot come out and tell you all," said Hillard. "I cannot compromise my honor."

But it wasn't long before Hillard let it slip that Ferrandini's group planned to draw ballots to decide who would kill Lincoln. When Pinkerton heard this news, he knew what their next move needed to be if they were going to save Lincoln's life.

Pinkerton told Davies that he needed to become a member of the Palmetto Guards so he could attend their secret meetings. It was a matter of life and death. Davies didn't delay.

He met with Hillard that day, and very carefully, he broached the idea of joining the Palmetto Guards. He told Hillard that he also wanted the opportunity to immortalize himself with the chance to murder Lincoln. Hillard believed his new friend and told him he'd see what he could do.

It didn't take long. Later that day, Hillard gave him the news. He'd put in a good word for Davies, vouching for him. He could join the Palmetto Guards—that night.

X

Candles flickered in a shadowy room where dozens of men were sitting in silence. When Davies walked into the secret meeting, he recognized many of the members of the Palmetto Guards. He had socialized with these wealthy men at Barnum's.

Davies was led to the front of the room, where Captain Cypriano Ferrandini, dressed in black, stood. The members formed a circle around Davies. Kneeling before Ferrandini,

Davies took the oath, swearing allegiance to their cause. Afterward, the members warmly shook Davies's hand, welcoming him to their secret military organization.

Quieting the group down, Ferrandini began to speak. Davies paid close attention while Ferrandini outlined the details of their plot to assassinate Lincoln.

The assassination was to take place at the Calvert Street train depot. A large crowd of secessionists would gather there. When Lincoln got off the train, several secessionists would create a diversion by getting into a large fight outside the depot. This would divert attention away from Lincoln, and the police would abandon him to go break up the fight.

With the police out of the picture, an angry mob would gather around Lincoln, giving the assassin an opportunity to get close and kill him.

Ferrandini drew his sword and held it over his head, exclaiming, "This hireling Lincoln shall never, never be president!"

Everyone cheered enthusiastically. And when the crowd quieted down, Ferrandini presented a box full of pieces of paper.

Just as Hillard had described, Ferrandini instructed each member of the Palmetto Guards to reach in the box and take a ballot. One of the ballots was colored red, and whoever picked the red ballot was Lincoln's killer.

Some of the candles were snuffed so the room was darker. That way, no one would know for sure who drew the red one.

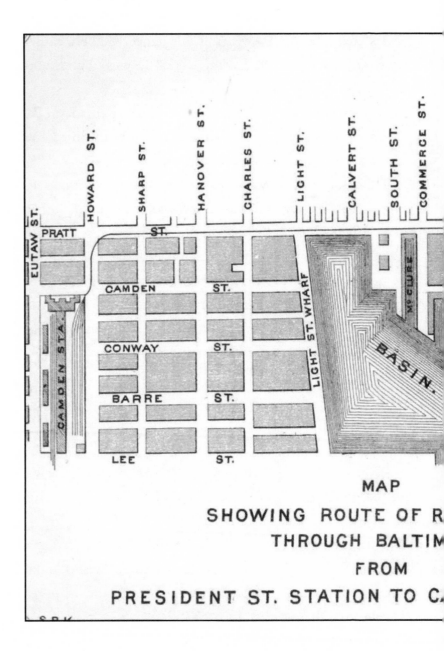

MAP

SHOWING ROUTE OF R

THROUGH BALTIM

FROM

PRESIDENT ST. STATION TO C

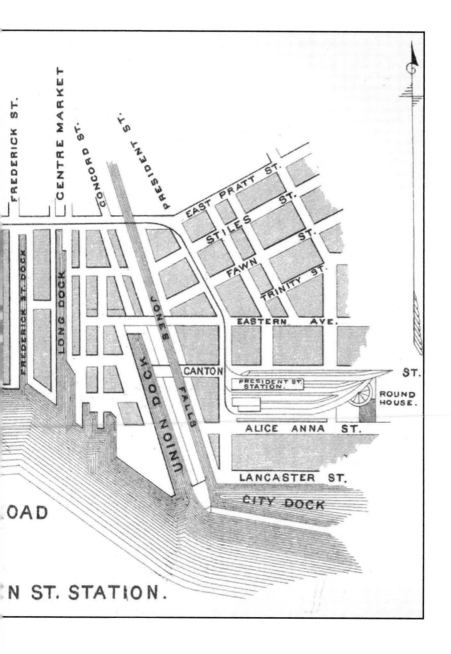

The men lined up, and each one reached in the box and picked a ballot.

Davies's ballot wasn't red, and neither was Hillard's. But Davies learned that to ensure the assassination of Lincoln, Ferrandini had secretly stuffed the ballot box. There wasn't one red ballot. There were eight.

So when Lincoln hopped off the train to meet and greet the people in Baltimore, eight assassins would be lurking in the crowd.

"My time for action," said Pinkerton, "had now arrived."

Chapter 3
Midnight Mission

Philadelphia, Pennsylvania, February 21, 1861
2 days before Lincoln's arrival in Baltimore

At 10:30 p.m., Pinkerton sat in a room in the Continental Hotel, located on the corner of Ninth and Chestnut Streets in Philadelphia. He heard a large and noisy crowd gathering outside the door. The door opened, and Abraham Lincoln walked in.

Lincoln immediately recognized Pinkerton. They had met several times when Lincoln was the lawyer for the Illinois Central Railroad, one of Pinkerton's biggest clients.

Lincoln's adviser, the ruddy-faced senator Norman Judd, who had been waiting with Pinkerton, briefly explained the reason for Pinkerton's late-night visit. Pinkerton didn't take his eyes off Lincoln as Judd informed him that the secessionists in Baltimore planned to murder him.

"Mr. Lincoln listened very attentively, but did not say a word . . . He appeared thoughtful and serious," said Pinkerton.

Pinkerton then offered a plan of action.

"During the time I was speaking," said Pinkerton, "Mr. Lincoln listened with great attention only asking a question occasionally."

After Pinkerton finished, Lincoln was quiet, mulling things over. He liked Pinkerton and had confidence in him. After carefully considering Pinkerton's plan of leaving that night and arriving in Washington ahead of schedule, Lincoln made a decision.

Abraham Lincoln, with his top hat nearby. His right hand is swollen after shaking hands all day.

"I didn't like it," said Lincoln. "I had made engagements to visit Harrisburg, and go from there to Baltimore, and I resolved to do so. I could not believe that there was a plot to murder me."

Pinkerton observed through the entire conversation that Lincoln showed no fear.

"Calm and self-possessed," Pinkerton said of Lincoln. "His only sentiments appeared to be those of profound regret, that the Southern sympathizers . . . consider[ed] his death a necessity for the furtherance of their cause."

Lincoln was firm in his decision. He was going to stay in Philadelphia. The next day he was scheduled to raise the flag over Independence Hall.

The flag-raising ceremony was intended to honor Kansas, which had been admitted to the Union as a free state after a long and bloody fight. The victory had to be marked, Lincoln felt. The rebels needed to see that he was determined to stand firm against the expansion of slavery.

And he wasn't going to change his plans to arrive in Harrisburg before making his way to Baltimore. After listening to Lincoln, Pinkerton knew it was pointless to try to change his mind.

But when Lincoln left the hotel room and was making his way through the crowded hallway, he ran into Frederick Seward, whose father, William, was a New York senator.

"He had been sent at the instance [sic] of his father and

General Scott," said Lincoln, "to inform me that their detectives in Baltimore had discovered a plot there to assassinate me. *They knew nothing of Mr. Pinkerton's movements.*"

Lincoln now believed a plot existed and agreed to leave for Baltimore early, but he insisted on keeping his promise to raise the flag in Philadelphia and visit Harrisburg.

"I shall endeavor to get away quietly from the people at Harrisburg tomorrow evening," Lincoln said to Pinkerton. "And shall place myself in your hands."

✕

At midnight Pinkerton met with Judd; George Franciscus, the general manager of the Pennsylvania Central Railroad; and Edward Sanford, president of the American Telegraph Company. Working through the night, they considered every possible scenario. No one got any sleep. But before dawn, they had a plan.

The next morning, February 22, at six o'clock, Lincoln raised the American flag over Independence Hall. Although he hadn't prepared a speech, Lincoln was filled with emotion, stating that all people are created equal.

"Now, my friends," he continued, "can this country be saved upon that basis? If it can, I will consider myself one of the happiest men in the world if I can help save it. If it cannot be saved upon that principle, it will be truly awful. But if this country cannot be saved without giving up that principle . . ."

Abraham Lincoln kept his promise to raise the flag at Independence Hall. Lincoln is standing near the center of the flag, without his top hat on.

Lincoln suddenly paused. His meeting with Pinkerton was on his mind.

"I was about to say I would rather be assassinated on this spot than surrender it. Now, in my view of the present aspect of affairs, there is no need of bloodshed and war. There is no necessity for it. I am not in favor of such a course, and I may say in advance that there will be no bloodshed unless it is forced upon the government."

When Lincoln finished his speech, the crowd cheered. Afterward, he boarded a train for Harrisburg.

In Harrisburg, Lincoln addressed a crowd of people from the balcony of the Jones House hotel. He then went to the statehouse and addressed a joint meeting of the general assembly. After lots of handshaking and greetings, Lincoln returned to his hotel.

Before Lincoln sat down for dinner at 4:30 p.m., he quietly informed a few trusted men about Pinkerton's plan.

Some were worried. They didn't trust Pinkerton. What if it was a trap? What if Pinkerton was really selling him to the secessionists? But Lincoln told them that he'd known Pinkerton for years and trusted him with his life.

At 5:45 p.m., a horse-drawn carriage pulled up to the side door of the hotel where Lincoln had just finished his dinner. At 6:00 p.m., Lincoln was supposed to excuse himself from the table and slip out the door. But it wasn't going to be easy.

The hotel was packed with people, and there was a big crowd outside the hotel. Bonfires were burning in the streets and people were shouting. Everyone wanted to catch a glimpse of Lincoln.

Even so, Lincoln stood up from his chair and excused himself from the table. Pretending to be tired, he took ahold of Governor Andrew Curtin's arm. The governor led Lincoln to his hotel room, where he grabbed his overnight bag. And then, following Pinkerton's instructions, he put on a disguise.

Lincoln always wore a black top hat. It not only made him look taller, but he was easy to spot in a crowd. That night, Lincoln left his top hat behind. Instead, he decided to take a soft wool hat—something he had never worn before.

"I put on an old overcoat that I had with me, and putting the soft hat in my pocket, I walked out of the house at a back door, bareheaded, without exciting a special curiosity," said Lincoln. "Then I put on the soft hat and joined my friends without being recognized by strangers, for I was not the same man."

✕

Two miles outside of Harrisburg, a trusted employee of the American Telegraph Company climbed a pole and cut the telegraph wires from Harrisburg to Baltimore. No one— not even a Southern spy—could send a message to alert the conspirators that Lincoln had left early.

×

At 9:15 p.m., a ciphered telegram arrived at the St. Louis Hotel in Philadelphia. It was addressed to "J. H. Hutchinson." When decoded, it read—

"Nuts left at six—Everything as you directed—all is right."

The telegram was signed by George H. Burns, a telegraph operator for the railroad. When Pinkerton finished reading it, he knew that Lincoln, code name Nuts, was on the train to Philadelphia.

×

At 9:45 p.m., a horse-drawn carriage stopped outside the Philadelphia train station. Kate Warne climbed out of the carriage and walked into the station, where she bought three train tickets to Washington, D.C.

×

At 10:03 p.m., in Philadelphia, Pinkerton was in a horse-drawn carriage with Lincoln. Lincoln's train from Harrisburg had arrived early. It was too dangerous to be seen at the train station, and Pinkerton wanted to time their arrival just right. So he had the driver take them in search of an imaginary person through Philadelphia.

Lincoln spoke quietly to Pinkerton. He mentioned that his wife, Mary, was not happy at all about his situation and insisted on traveling with him. She reluctantly agreed with Pinkerton's plan.

When the carriage finally arrived at the PW&B train station, Kate Warne greeted Lincoln and, as part of the cover, acted like he was her brother. While they quickly and stealthily stepped into the train through the back door, one of Pinkerton's contacts brought an official and very important-looking package to the conductor.

When the conductor received the package, he knew that it was okay to leave the train station. Mr. Felton, the president of the PW&B Railroad, was expecting it, and the conductor was told that under no circumstance should the train leave until the package was received. In truth, the package was really a safeguard in Pinkerton's plan to ensure the train wouldn't leave without Lincoln on it. Inside the package was just a bunch of old railroad reports.

✕

A few minutes later, the whistle sounded, and the train began to rumble down the tracks. Pinkerton still feared that plotters might destroy the railroad tracks. But for now, Lincoln, Pinkerton, and the others were safely in the narrow sleeping berth, sitting on the padded bench that was to be his bed for the night. A flimsy curtain divided them from the other passengers.

"He talked very friendly for some time," said Warne.

Inside a train's sleeping car.

"We all went to bed early. Mr. Pinkerton did not sleep, nor did Mr. Lincoln. The excitement seemed to keep us all awake."

Warne also noted another reason Lincoln couldn't sleep. Lincoln was "so very tall that he could not lay straight in his berth."

✕

When the train approached Havre de Grace, Maryland, about thirty-five miles from Baltimore, Pinkerton went outside and stood on the rear platform of the train car. As the train thundered down the tracks, he looked into the darkness and saw a bright lantern light flash, two times. It was exactly what he was looking for—a secret signal from his undercover agent Timothy Webster, telling Pinkerton "All's well!"

From this point until they arrived in Baltimore, Pinkerton had an undercover agent at every bridge crossing. As the train rumbled by, Pinkerton kept a steady watch for the flashing lights, signaling "All's well!"

It was 3:30 a.m. when the train reached Baltimore. As instructed by Pinkerton, Kate Warne got off the train to stay behind in Baltimore. Her assignment was to keep her eyes and ears open for any talk about Lincoln and his change of plans.

Pinkerton climbed out of the sleeping berth, got off the train, and was standing on the depot when he heard the words whispered in his ear, "All's well!" before getting back on the train.

Two hours later the train whistle blew and headed for Washington.

✕

When the train screeched to a halt in Washington, D.C., at six o'clock in the morning, Lincoln wrapped a shawl around his shoulders and, accompanied by Pinkerton, stepped off the train.

As Lincoln walked onto the crowded platform, Pinkerton followed closely behind him. Suddenly, a man stepped out from behind the pillar. He seized upon Lincoln, grabbing his arm.

"Abe, you can't play that on me," the man said, referring to Lincoln's disguise.

The man was right next to Pinkerton, and Pinkerton punched him with his elbow. The man staggered back but quickly recovered. The man grabbed Lincoln again, saying he knew him. Pinkerton drew back his fist, aiming to strike a blow.

"Don't strike him, Allan, don't strike him," said Lincoln, grabbing Pinkerton's arm. "That's my friend Washburne—don't you know him?"

Fearing someone would recognize Lincoln, Pinkerton stood between the two men and said, "No talking here!"

Pinkerton could see the resentment in Congressman Elihu Washburne's eyes.

Congressman Elihu Washburne found out the hard way that it's best not to surprise Allan Pinkerton while he's on the job.

"That is Mr. Pinkerton, and everything is all right," said Lincoln, smoothing things over with his friend who was there to meet them.

Washburne led them to a carriage that was waiting for them outside. Lincoln was whisked away safely to the Willard Hotel.

✕

At 12:30 p.m., at the Baltimore train depot, thousands of people were waiting for the arrival of Abraham Lincoln's train. One of the people anxiously waiting was Otis Hillard, the regular at Barnum's Hotel. That day, he proudly wore the gold palmetto badge on the outside of his vest. But he soon realized that the rumors were true—Lincoln had already traveled through Baltimore in the middle of the night.

"How in Hell [had] it leaked out that Lincoln was to be mobbed in Baltimore?" Hillard said to Harry Davies.

Surprisingly, none of the plotters were ever arrested.

"Finding that their plans had been discovered," said Pinkerton, "and fearing that the vengeance of the government were to overtake them, the leading conspirators had suddenly disappeared. All their courage and bravado was gone, and now, like the miserable cowards that they were, they had sought safety in flight."

Chapter 4
At Your Secret Service

Washington, D.C., March 4, 1861
The day of Abraham Lincoln's presidential inauguration

It was a cold and dreary day. Heavy dark clouds hung in the sky, threatening to rain on Abraham Lincoln's presidential inauguration. Despite the forbidding weather, thousands of people crowded the streets in Washington, D.C., to see Abraham Lincoln sworn in as president.

Riflemen and sharpshooters from the army stood guard, ready to fire from the windows and rooftops, and a large special police force patrolled the streets while Lincoln gave his speech during the ceremony. In a loud and clear voice, he spoke about the rising conflict and widening divide between the Northern and Southern states.

"In your hands, my dissatisfied fellow-country-men, and not in mine, is the momentous issue of civil war," Lincoln said. "The Government will not assail you. You can have no conflict without being yourselves the aggressors . . . We are not enemies, but friends. We must not be enemies."

President Abraham Lincoln at his inauguration.

One of Lincoln's first orders of business as president of the United States was to send supplies to Fort Sumter, a military post on an island off the coast of Charleston, South Carolina. Major Robert Anderson and his men had been holed up there since December. At that time, South Carolina had seceded from the Union and pointed their guns at the fort. It was a standoff. Anderson and his men had steadfastly refused to surrender, but they were running out of food.

Not wanting to show aggression toward South Carolina, Lincoln informed the Confederates that he was sending only food and not reinforcements. He told them it was a humanitarian mission.

Six days later, on April 12, the Confederates fired the first shot at Fort Sumter. Outnumbered and outgunned, three and a half days later, Anderson finally surrendered. The Civil War had begun.

✕

About two weeks later, Pinkerton spy Timothy Webster had a dire problem. Pinkerton had entrusted him to carry important documents that needed to be delivered to President Lincoln in Washington, D.C. The trouble was how to get them there.

Webster had taken the train from Chicago all the way to Perrymansville, Maryland. But from that point on, the trains weren't running.

With the fall of Fort Sumter into the Confederates' hands, Lincoln declared that Washington, D.C., "was put into the condition of a siege." Located inside the slave state of Maryland, the nation's capital was essentially defenseless. And it was feared that the Confederates were on their way to invade and capture Washington, D.C.

On April 14, Lincoln called for seventy-five thousand Union volunteer troops to hurry to Washington to protect it from the Confederates. But on April 19, when some of the Northern troops changed trains in Baltimore, they were greeted by an angry mob.

Screaming insults and hurling bottles, stones, and bricks at the Union soldiers, a riot broke out. Bullets were fired. Four soldiers were killed, and thirty-six were wounded.

To prevent more Northern troops from traveling through Baltimore, the mayor and governor ordered the Baltimore County Horse Guards to burn all the bridges and destroy the railroad tracks. The telegraph wires were also cut.

The *Baltimore Sun* reported that "armed men [are] stationed everywhere, determined to give the Northern troops a fight in their march to the capital."

Washington, D.C., was now cut off from the North. Pinkerton's spy Timothy Webster had managed to take a rowboat across the Susquehanna River to Havre de Grace, Maryland. But he was still seventy-five miles away from Washington. Since he couldn't take the train, he needed to find a way to get there. So Webster went to a hotel and asked the hotelkeeper.

"I do not know," said the hotelkeeper. "This gentleman is anxious to do the same thing."

The gentleman was tall, standing ramrod straight. From the moment Webster first laid eyes on him, he suspected the man was hiding something. He had shifty eyes.

"Yes, I am very anxious to get through," the man said with a British accent. "I am a bearer of dispatches to the British Consul at Washington, and it is of the utmost importance that they should be delivered at once."

As he was talking, a team of horses pulled up to the hotel. Webster and the Englishman offered to pay a wagon driver fifty dollars to take them to Baltimore. It was a lot of money, and the wagon driver agreed to take them.

Webster thought the long ride would be the perfect opportunity to find out what the Englishman was really up to. But the Englishman barely spoke to him—until they were stopped by a soldier on horseback outside of Perrymansville, Maryland.

"Who are you, and where are you going?" the soldier demanded.

Webster recognized the soldier's uniform. It was the same one he'd worn when he worked undercover in Perrymansville during the Lincoln assassination plot. However, he didn't recognize the soldier.

"We are residents of Baltimore," Webster said. "And we are endeavoring to get home."

"You will have to go with me," the soldier said. "You can't go any further without permission."

Webster hid any uneasiness he was feeling about getting caught. After traveling a short distance with the armed soldier, another Confederate soldier approached their wagon. Relief washed over him. Webster knew him from Perrymansville.

"Hello, Taylor!" Webster said to the soldier. "How are you?"

Taylor looked into the wagon and saluted him.

"Why, Webster, how do you do?" said Taylor. "The boys said you would not come back, now that the war had commenced, but I knew better, and I am glad to see you."

"Oh yes," said Webster. "I have come back; and my friend here and I are anxious to get to Baltimore as soon as possible."

"That will be all right," said Taylor. He turned to the soldier who had stopped them and said, "These men are all right; you will permit them to pass."

Taylor handed Webster a pass, in case they were stopped again.

After this incident, Webster noticed the Englishman looked relieved. Webster wondered what he was hiding. He suspected he wasn't delivering documents for the British Consul.

As they traveled to Baltimore, the Englishman engaged Webster in a friendly conversation. This was a sudden change in his demeanor, and Webster suspected that the Englishman believed he was a Confederate. So Webster hinted to the Englishman that he was.

It worked. Webster had gained his trust. Soon the Englishman confided in Webster that he was carrying important military dispatches for Southern sympathizers in Washington, D.C.

Webster responded by shaking the man's hand warmly, greeting him as a fellow patriot. When they reached Baltimore, they had dinner together and smoked cigars.

The next morning, they paid another fifty dollars to a driver with two horses and traveled to Washington, D.C. However, right before the horse-drawn wagon took off, Webster asked if he would wait a moment. He had forgotten something in his hotel room.

The driver and the Englishman waited patiently. While inside the hotel, Webster took a pen and wrote a note. He folded the note up and tucked it into his pocket.

When Webster returned, the wagon headed out. By noontime, they were several miles outside of Washington, D.C. It was very hot, and the horses were tired, so they stopped at the Twelve-Mile House, where they had lunch.

While Webster was eating his meal, he recognized a man who he'd been friends with years ago. The man was wearing a Union uniform and was a lieutenant. Webster avoided making eye contact with him and went unrecognized.

When Webster finished eating, he saw his old friend get up from the table. Webster excused himself. He walked out to the hallway where he found him.

They spoke quietly for a few minutes, and Webster discreetly handed him the note from his pocket. Then he returned to the table to have a cigar with the Englishman.

Afterward, Webster and the Englishman climbed back into the wagon and started the last leg of their journey. As they approached Washington, D.C., a Union lieutenant with eight soldiers emerged from a building and halted their wagon.

"Gentlemen, I am sorry to discommode you," said the lieutenant. "But I have orders to intercept all persons entering the city and hold them until they can satisfactorily account for themselves. You will be kind enough to consider yourselves under arrest and follow me."

Webster and the Englishman both looked stunned. But they followed the lieutenant into a building that was used as a military guardhouse. Once inside, the Englishman watched the lieutenant lock Webster in a room before he was locked up.

A few minutes later, the lieutenant quietly turned the key, unlocking Webster's door and releasing him.

Webster thanked the lieutenant, who was his old friend that he had spoken to earlier in the hallway at the Twelve-Mile House. When Webster had handed his friend the note, it read:

To Whom It May Concern

My companion is an emissary of the Confederacy, carrying dispatches to Southern sympathizers in Washington. Apprehend him, but do so discreetly and without compromising me.

T.W.

Less than a half an hour later, Webster was walking up the steps of the White House. He was soon standing before President Lincoln. Webster took his coat off, ripped open the lining, and pulled out a dozen important documents—letters and dispatches from Chicago. Lincoln watched quietly but with amused interest.

"You have brought quite a mail with you, Mr. Webster," said Lincoln. "More, perhaps, than it would be quite safe to attempt to carry another time."

"Yes, sir," said Webster. "I don't think I would like to carry so much through Baltimore another time."

Lincoln carefully looked over the documents. One of the letters was from Pinkerton. It read:

Dear Sir,

When I saw you last I said that if the time should ever come that I could be of service to you I was ready. If that time has come I am on hand.

I have in my Force from sixteen to eighteen

persons on whose courage, skill, and devotion to their country I can rely. If they, with myself at the head, can be at service in any way of obtaining information of the movements of traitors, or safely conveying your letters or dispatches, or that class of Secret Service, which is most dangerous, I am at your command.

In the present disturbed state of affairs I dare not trust this to mail. So send by one of my Force who was with me in Baltimore. You may safely trust him with any message for me. Written or verbal. I fully guarantee his fidelity. He will act as you direct and return here with your answer.

Secrecy is the great lever I propose to operate with—Hence the necessity of this movement (If you contemplate it) being kept Strictly Private, and that should you desire another interview with the Bearer that you should so arrange it as that he will not be noticed.

The Bearer will hand you a copy of a telegraphic cipher which you may use if you desire to telegraph me—

My Force comprises both sexes. All of Good Character. And well skilled in their business.

Respectfully yours,

Allan Pinkerton

Confidential

Chicago April 21st 1861

To His Excellency
A Lincoln
Prest of the U.S.

Dear Sir

When I saw you last I said that if the time should ever come that I could be of service to you I was ready. If that time has come I am on hand.

I have in my Force from Sixteen to Eighteen persons on whose courage, Skill & Devotion to their Country I can rely. If they, with myself at the head can be of service in the way of obtaining information of the Movements of the Traitors, or Safely conveying your letters or dispatches, or that class of Secret Service which is the Most dangerous. I am at your command.

In the present disturbed state of affairs I dare not trust this to the Mail. So send by one of My Force who was with me at Baltimore. You may safely trust him with any Message for me—Written or Verbal. I fully guarantee his fidelity. He will act as you direct, and return here with your answer

Secrecy is the great lever I propose

Pinkerton's letter to President Lincoln offering his spy network of "Secret Service."

to Operate with – Hence the necessity of this movement (If you contemplate it) being kept Strictly Private. and that should you desire another interview with the Bearer that you should so arrange it. as that he will not be noticed –

The Bearer will hand you a Copy of a Telegraph Cipher which you may use if you desire to Telegraph me –

My Force comprises both Sexes. all of good Character. and well Skilled in their Business.

Respectfully yours
Allan Pinkerton

After looking over the documents, Lincoln decided he needed some time to think things over, even though he and his Cabinet members had for some time been mulling over the idea of creating an intelligence-gathering organization.

"Mr. Webster, I have a Cabinet conference this evening, and I will not be able to give these matters my attention until tomorrow. Come to me at ten o'clock and I will see you at that time."

The following morning, Webster went to the White House and stood before President Lincoln, carrying a cane.

"Mr. Webster, you have rendered the country an invaluable service," said Lincoln. "The bearer of dispatches who was arrested last evening by your efforts, proved, as you suspected, to be an emissary of the South, and the letters found upon him disclose a state of affairs quite alarming. Several prominent families here are discovered to be in regular communication with the Southern leaders and are furnishing them with every item of information."

Lincoln handed Webster some telegrams.

"When you have reached a point where communication is possible, send them to General McClellan, at Columbus, Ohio," said Lincoln.

McClellan was an old friend of Lincoln's and Pinkerton's. He had been the vice president and engineer in chief of the Illinois Central Railroad. It was through McClellan that Pinkerton had first met Lincoln when Lincoln was the railroad's lawyer.

McClellan was now in command of Ohio's state militia and would soon be in command of the combined military Union troops from Ohio, Indiana, and Illinois, called the Department of Ohio. His objective was to occupy western Virginia, which wanted to remain in the Union.

Lincoln had one more thing to ask of Webster.

"Also, telegraph to Mr. Pinkerton to come to Washington," said Lincoln. "His services are, I think, greatly needed by the government at this time."

Webster rolled up the telegrams, removed the handle of his cane, and slid the papers into its hollow center. Once the documents were safely hidden, Webster left the White House.

It would soon be time for Pinkerton to spearhead the Union Intelligence Service—or what Pinkerton called the Secret Service.

Chapter 5
A Sharp-Dressed Man

Cincinnati, Ohio, May 1861

Soon after Timothy Webster had hand delivered Pinkerton's letter to President Lincoln offering to organize the Secret Service, General McClellan contacted Pinkerton and put him in charge of a "secret service force" for his army.

"This was the first real organization of the Secret Service," said Pinkerton.

The headquarters were set up in an office building in downtown Cincinnati. Pinkerton brought along his most experienced operatives. His first order of business from McClellan was to cross enemy lines and gather military information about the bordering Confederate states. Pinkerton sent Webster to Louisville, Kentucky, and on to Memphis, Tennessee.

"In Webster's case it was not necessary to devote much time to instructions, except as to his line of travel, for he was a man who understood the whole meaning of a mission like this," said Pinkerton.

Major General George B. McClellan.

Still posing as a Confederate from Maryland, Webster made friends with Confederate officers in Memphis. They even gave him a guided tour of the city's defenses. Webster sent back a detailed report.

George Bangs continued to work as Pinkerton's right-hand man, overseeing the day-to-day operations in Cincinnati. This allowed Pinkerton to go undercover behind enemy lines. McClellan wanted information "on the general feeling of the people" in Kentucky, North Carolina, Mississippi, and Louisiana.

Using the alias E. J. Allen, which he would use throughout the war, Pinkerton posed as a gentleman from Georgia. Traveling alone on horseback, Pinkerton also gathered information about the conditions of the roads, the number of bridges, the number of troops, and the types of weapons he saw along the way.

When he returned to Cincinnati, it wasn't long before his detective Pryce Lewis arrived from Tennessee. Lewis hadn't been on a mission for the Secret Service. Instead, he'd been working on a murder investigation, his first big case for Pinkerton. Lewis had been on the case since April, before the start of the Civil War. He planned on reporting the details of the case to Pinkerton in person before returning to Chicago. But Pinkerton had something else in mind for him.

McClellan needed more information about the locations of the Confederate fortifications in Virginia. He was planning to oust the Confederates in western Virginia. Pinkerton knew just the person for the job. He wanted Lewis to go undercover in Virginia, posing as an English nobleman.

Lewis wasn't English. He was Welsh. He had also grown up in abject poverty, being the son of an illiterate weaver. But that didn't matter. Pinkerton made sure Lewis looked the part of an aristocrat—expensive clothes, the finest horses and carriage, and the best cigars and champagne. Pinkerton even loaned him his gold watch and diamond ring. Lewis would also be traveling with a "servant." Pinkerton assigned his other operative, Sam Bridgeman, who was originally from Virginia, to the task.

Pleased with his convincing disguise, the charismatic and confident Lewis decided to call himself Lord Tracy. He was ready for the mission to begin.

X

When a patrol of Confederate cavalrymen halted an elegant-looking carriage along the James River and Kanawha Turnpike in western Virginia, they were surprised to find an English nobleman napping inside. He was dressed up in an expensive suit with a silk top hot, and his gold watch and diamond ring sparkled in the sunlight. The sergeant demanded to see his pass.

Irritated for being rudely awakened, Pryce Lewis told them that he wasn't aware that a vacationing Englishman needed a pass to travel through the South. Lewis was promptly taken to a nearby farmhouse for questioning.

Pryce Lewis, the spy in a top hat.

At the farmhouse, a young officer introduced himself as Colonel Patton, the Confederate's commanding officer of the 1st Kanawha Infantry Regiment. Patton was in charge of defending the forty miles of turnpike from the small town of Guyandotte to Charleston in western Virginia.

Pryce Lewis introduced himself as Lord Tracy and informed Patton that he was taking a grand tour of the South. He wanted to see the sights, such as the Natural Bridge, which was on the way to Richmond. Lewis complained bitterly about needing a pass.

"My good sir," said Patton. "We have no intention to stop Englishmen from traveling in our country."

Patton gave Lewis a pass. Cheered, Lewis asked Patton if he'd like a cigar. While they smoked, he asked Patton if he would like some champagne. Patton laughed, thinking it was a joke. Champagne was not easy to come by with the war going on.

Pinkerton's spy Sam Bridgeman, posing as the servant and driver of the carriage, quickly retrieved a bottle from a silver-embossed box. While drinking champagne, Lewis and Patton talked in general terms about the ongoing war. After a couple of glasses, Patton mentioned that the location of their camp, named Camp Tompkins, was ten miles from Charleston, Virginia.

Patton then asked Lewis if he had encountered any Union soldiers in the area during his travels. Lewis said he had indeed but was quick to assure Patton that he was very unimpressed by them.

The news that Union soldiers were close to the area didn't surprise Patton. He confided to Lewis that he had fortifications here.

"With nine hundred Confederate soldiers I can defend against ten thousand Yankees for ten years," said Patton.

Lewis mentioned that the fortifications he'd seen during his time as a soldier in the Crimean War were impressive. In truth, Lewis was never a soldier, but the lie was convincing. When Patton learned that Lewis had been a soldier, he insisted that Lewis stay for dinner.

Lewis gladly accepted the invitation. He would worry later about how he was going to get back safely to Cincinnati and report all the details to Pinkerton.

✕

After meeting Colonel Patton, Lewis and Bridgeman decided to take their chances and gather more information in Charleston, Virginia. Once there, Lewis checked into the Kanawha Hotel, right across the hall from Confederate general Henry Wise, the person in charge of the western Virginia military.

For the next ten days, Lewis drank champagne and smoked cigars with Confederate officers. He entertained them with stories of his time spent fighting in the Crimean

War—taken straight from the pages of his favorite book, *The History of the War with Russia*. The Confederate soldiers liked him so much that they gave him a tour of Camp Tompkins, where Lewis noted the number of soldiers, the amount of rations, and the type of weapons, among other details.

The only person who wasn't impressed with Lewis was General Wise. This was bad news for Lewis and Bridgeman. Wise routinely rounded up and arrested any suspected Union men. The town's jail was overflowing with them. So when Wise invited Lewis to his room, it wasn't to socialize—it was to interrogate him.

"Lord Tracy" stood his ground with Wise, never once breaking from character. Nevertheless, Lewis was shaken. He and Bridgeman needed to get out of town.

But Lewis was worried if they left immediately, it would show their guilt. Also, if anyone saw them heading north, they risked arrest.

While drinking in the saloons and mingling with the townsfolk and soldiers, Bridgeman had learned about the rough back roads that headed north. It was unlikely they would run into any Confederate soldiers. Even so, there was still the problem of raising suspicion by leaving.

Lewis decided to sleep on it. But it was a sleepless night; Lewis was riddled with anxiety. After midnight, he was startled to hear a knock on Wise's door. Lewis walked quietly to his door and tried to eavesdrop. All he could hear was Wise say, "Call Colonel Tompkins."

Confederate General Henry A. Wise.

Soon after, Lewis heard Wise leave his room. The next morning Lewis found out that Wise and many of his soldiers had left. McClellan's troops were advancing from Parkersburg, Virginia, heading toward them. Wise was going to meet them with his Confederate troops.

It was a stroke of luck for Lewis and Bridgeman. They saw their opportunity to leave town without Wise's knowledge. They told the hotelkeeper that they were heading south to Richmond. But once they were out of sight, they turned and headed north, taking the back roads.

McClellan would receive their valuable information just in the nick of time.

✕

Pryce Lewis's information was so valuable that McClellan ordered him to deliver it personally to Brigadier General Jacob Cox, who was in charge of capturing Charleston, Virginia. Lewis met with Cox on July 21, 1861.

The next day, on July 22, Cox attacked Wise's troops. Cox knew, based on Lewis's report, that he had more troops and was better equipped. On July 24, Wise and his Confederate soldiers fled, abandoning western Virginia. The Union had successfully taken back western Virginia. Splitting the state of Virginia in two, the newly created state of West Virginia was added to the Union.

Not long after, Lincoln summoned McClellan to Washington, D.C. He replaced Colonel Thomas A. Scott with

McClellan, promoting him to the overall commander of the Union army.

McClellan brought Pinkerton and his Secret Service to Washington, D.C. One of Pinkerton's first assignments was to capture a well-known socialite and Confederate spy whose nickname was Rebel Rose.

Chapter 6
Rebel Rose

Washington, D.C., August 1861

It wasn't the best weather for spying. The rain was falling furiously from the night sky. The pounding drops of water soaked Pinkerton's clothes, and the harsh wind chilled him. A gas light was shining through the blinds from the second-story window into the parlor—the largest and grandest room in the brick home that was located just a few blocks away from the White House. Inside the house was a suspected Confederate spy.

Removing his wet boots, Pinkerton stood in his bare feet on the shoulders of Pryce Lewis and Sam Bridgeman. He couldn't see a thing through the window. But that wasn't going to stop him.

He quietly opened the window, reached his hand inside, and turned the slats of the blind. He now had a full view of the fancy furniture, valuable paintings, and statues that furnished the parlor. But no one was in the room. Just as he was about to express his disappointment, he was interrupted.

"Shh!" said one of his operatives.

Someone was walking toward the house. Pinkerton quickly got down from their shoulders, and they hid under the stoop that led to the front door. They heard the footsteps go up the stairs and the doorbell ring. The cold rain kept falling, but they ignored their discomfort.

They ran back to the parlor window and propped Pinkerton on their shoulders. He peered into the window and recognized the handsome Union army officer. He was Captain John Elwood, who was in charge of a military police station. Elwood sat nervously in a chair—until the vivacious socialite Rose Greenhow swept into the room.

His face brightened, and he stood up from his chair. Rose Greenhow cordially welcomed him into her home. He gave her a courtly bow.

Soon, Captain Elwood and Mrs. Greenhow were seated at a table and were talking. But they were talking softly and the wind was so loud, Pinkerton could catch only pieces of their conversation. But he heard enough to know that the Captain was giving Mrs. Greenhow information about the Union troops.

Pinkerton watched as Captain Elwood took a map out of his coat pocket and held it up to the light. He could see that it was a map of the planned fortifications in and around Washington, D.C., in anticipation of a Confederate attack.

"My blood boiled with indignation as I witnessed this

scene," said Pinkerton. "And I longed to rush into the room and strangle the miscreant."

But Pinkerton kept standing on his operatives' shoulders, keeping watch, and waiting patiently for Elwood to leave. It was 12:30 a.m. when he finally heard the front door open. Pinkerton climbed down from the window. He heard Captain Elwood and Mrs. Greenhow whisper, "Good night," and kiss.

"Without paying any attention to the fact that I was without shoes, I started in pursuit of him," said Pinkerton. "And through the blinding mist and pelting storms kept him in view as he rapidly walked away."

Pinkerton followed quietly behind, but Elwood turned and looked around—not once but twice. He knew someone was following him, and he started to run. Pinkerton ran after him. When they reached a building with a guard nearby, Elwood disappeared inside. Before Pinkerton had time to stop and turn around, four armed guards ran toward him with their bayonets pointed at his chest.

"Halt, or I fire!" said a guard.

Pinkerton knew it wasn't a good idea to try to escape. He did try to tell them he was lost, but they didn't listen.

A half an hour later, a guard led Pinkerton to Elwood's room. When he entered, Elwood stopped pacing and stood in front of Pinkerton and glared at him.

"I was a sorry figure to look at," said Pinkerton. "And as I surveyed my weather-soaked and mud-stained garments, and my bare feet, I could scarcely repress a laugh, although

I was deeply angered at the sudden and unexpected turn affairs had taken."

Elwood demanded to know Pinkerton's name.

"E. J. Allen," he lied.

"What is your business?"

"I have nothing further to say," said Pinkerton. "And I decline to answer any further questions."

✕

Pinkerton's refusal to answer questions and reveal his true identity was a rule he established and expected all of his spies to follow in the newly created Secret Service. Only

Union Colonel Thomas A. Scott.

Lincoln, McClellan, and his spies knew that E. J. Allen was really Allan Pinkerton.

Since Pinkerton couldn't tell the officer he was part of the Secret Service, the officer had no choice.

"Take this man to the guardhouse," said Elwood. "But allow no one whatever to converse with him; we will attend further to his case in the morning."

Pinkerton was caught, but he managed to bribe a prison guard into delivering a note to Thomas A. Scott, the assistant secretary of war. The note told Scott about Pinkerton's imprisonment and asked for his release without causing suspicion. Even so, he spent a cold, miserable night in a prison cell.

The following morning, Elwood was called into Colonel Thomas A. Scott's office. Pinkerton was there, too, and he noticed right away the look on Elwood's face. Elwood was worried.

"Captain," said Colonel Scott, "will you give me the particulars of the arrest of this man?" He pointed to Pinkerton.

Captain Elwood said he'd been visiting friends, and when he was returning home, he thought a thief was following him.

"Did you see anyone last evening who is inimical to the cause of the government?"

Elwood hesitated. He gave a nervous glance to Pinkerton before answering.

"No, sir."

"Are you quite sure of that?" asked Colonel Scott.

"I am, sir."

But Pinkerton had already told Colonel Scott what he'd seen the night before through Greenhow's window. Colonel Scott knew Elwood was lying and guilty of supplying military information to Greenhow—a treasonable act against the Union.

"In that case, Captain, you will please consider yourself under arrest, and you will at once surrender your sword," said Colonel Scott.

They searched Captain Elwood's belongings and found evidence to prove he was giving information to the Confederates. They knew that he wasn't the first or the only leak of information.

"Mrs. Greenhow must be attended to. She is becoming a dangerous character," said Colonel Scott to Pinkerton. "You will there maintain your watch upon her, and should she be detected in attempting to convey any information outside of the lines, she must be arrested at once."

Chapter 7
Every Rose Has a Thorn

Washington, D.C., August 1861

From the outside looking in, wealthy widow Rose Greenhow appeared to be just another pretty face whose only concern was being the life of the party. A great conversationalist, especially if it was about politics, Greenhow was always the perfect hostess.

Her house buzzed with nearly constant activity—friends, family, and new acquaintances coming and going, day and night. Greenhow's parties were not to be missed. Her guest list always included powerful people. She counted former president James Buchanan, Confederate president Jefferson Davis, and former First Lady Dolly Madison among her many friends.

Even though she was living in Washington, D.C., the capital of the Union, Greenhow fiercely supported the newly formed Confederacy. But this wasn't unusual in Washington, D.C., which was teeming with Southern sympathizers who some called copperheads.

Rebel Rose Greenhow.

Despite Greenhow's open allegiance to the Southern cause, the vivacious and glamorous widow remained a very popular hostess with Confederates and Unionists. Many didn't suspect Greenhow's true intentions.

"Instead of friends, I see in those statesmen of Washington only mortal enemies," said Greenhow. "Instead of loving and worshipping the old flag of the Stars and Stripes, I see in it only the symbol of murder, plunder, oppression, and shame!"

So when the Civil War broke out, and Thomas Jordan, a US Army officer who later became a Confederate brigadier general, asked Greenhow to be part of the spy ring of women that he was organizing, she was enthusiastic. Greenhow invited her fellow spies to her parties so they, too, could use their charm to obtain information.

And when she successfully obtained information, she used a simple, twenty-six-symbol cipher that Jordan had shown her, so she could send him coded messages.

In early July 1861, just a month before Pinkerton began shadowing her, Rose picked up her first important piece of information. She gave a coded message to a teenager named Bettie Duval. Disguising herself as a farm girl, Duval rode a farm cart past the Union guards on the Chain Bridge across the Potomac River into Virginia. Once there, Duval changed into horseback riding clothes, borrowed a horse, and rode all the way to the Fairfax County Court House, a Confederate outpost that was keeping watch on the Union's movements. She told Confederate brigadier general Milledge Bonham that she had an important message for Confederate general P. G. T. Beauregard.

"Upon my announcing that I would have it faithfully forwarded at once," said Bonham, "she took out her tucking comb and let fall the longest and most beautiful roll of hair I have ever seen. She took then from the back of her head, where it had been safely tied, a small package, not larger than a silver dollar, sewed up in silk."

Inside was a coded message informing them when the Union army planned to advance toward them in

Rose Greenhow's seized ciphered letter.

31st July

All is activity. McClelland is busy night and day. but the panic is great and the attack is hourly expected. They believe that the attack will be made simultaneous from Edwards Ferry and Baltimore. Every effort is being made to find out who gave the alarm. A troop of Cavalry will start from here this Morning to Harpers Ferry. dont give time for re-organizing.

Rose Greenhow's ciphered letter decoded.

Manassas, Virginia, near Bull Run Creek. Greenhow sent a second coded message giving them the size of the Union army troops that were heading toward them. Even though her information wasn't always accurate, it was helpful. And with this information in hand, Confederate General Beauregard called for more troops and won the Battle of Bull Run.

A few days after the Battle of Bull Run, Greenhow received a dispatch. It read:

> Our President (Davis) and our General (Beauregard) direct me to thank you. We rely upon you for further information. The Confederacy owes you a debt.
> (Signed) Jordan, Adjutant-General

Greenhow was a force to be reckoned with. Pinkerton summed her up as possessing "an almost superhuman power, all of which she has most wickedly used to destroy the government."

But unlike Pinkerton, whose strategy was to remain anonymous and in the shadows, focusing on the secrecy of the operation, Greenhow wasn't so discreet. She and her fellow spies bragged and word soon reached the War Department. About a month after the Battle of Bull Run, the assistant secretary of war told Pinkerton to capture Rebel Rose.

✕

When Rose Greenhow left her house on Friday, August 23, she acted like she was taking a leisurely stroll through her neighborhood. She stopped at a neighbor's house to ask about their sick children, and as Greenhow continued her walk, she chatted with her neighbors. One neighbor told her that a guard was stationed outside her house all night long. Another told her she was being followed.

When she looked around, Greenhow noticed Pinkerton and an officer of the Union army standing near her house.

"Those men will probably arrest me," said Greenhow to a friend.

She was right. By watching her house, day and night, Pinkerton and his spies noticed a prominent attorney stopped by her house almost every night. He stayed a long time. Pinkerton discovered that the attorney had a network of men and women who relayed the messages Greenhow gave him across enemy lines.

Before Greenhow walked back to her house, she told her friend that if she was arrested, she would give a signal. The signal was raising a handkerchief to her face. She then put an important note in her mouth and ate it, destroying any evidence she had on herself.

She walked to her house and up the steps. As she was opening the door, Pinkerton and the officer approached her, asking if she was Mrs. Greenhow. She told them she was.

"Who are you, and what do you want?" she asked.

Pinkerton told her she was under arrest. Greenhow raised the handkerchief to her face before going inside her house.

"What are you going to do?" she asked.

"To search," said Pinkerton.

Greenhow was taken to her parlor, where Pryce Lewis stood guard, not allowing her to leave. Greenhow was furious but she wasn't about to show it. Instead, she turned on her charm.

While Pinkerton and his men searched her house, Greenhow chatted to Lewis, complaining sweetly about the intense summer heat. She followed up by asking him if she could go upstairs and change her clothes.

"She asked in such a winning way," said Lewis, so he agreed but insisted that he go with her.

He followed her up the stairs. As soon as Greenhow was inside her bedroom, she grabbed her revolver from the mantel over the fireplace. She spun around and pointed it at Lewis.

Lewis smiled. Then he told her that the revolver had to be cocked before it fired.

The gun was quickly taken away from Greenhow. Then Lewis left her alone to change, which is exactly what she wanted.

As soon as he left, Greenhow reached in her pocket and took out the papers with the cipher she used to send messages to General Thomas Jordan. She tore them up. Not long after, one of Pinkerton's woman operatives arrived to search Greenhow.

Rose Greenhow and her daughter at the Old Capitol Prison in Washington, D.C., in 1862.

"Her image is daguerreotyped on my mind," said Greenhow. "And as it is an ugly picture, I would willingly obliterate it."

Despite her unhappiness, Greenhow removed her elegant silk dress and handed it to the woman operative. While Greenhow stood in her corset, the woman operative examined the dress, looking for hidden papers.

For several days, Pinkerton and his operatives searched the house. They looked through every single book, page by page; took apart the furniture and framed paintings; and checked every nook and cranny. It paid off.

Pinkerton's operatives found the torn-up cipher she used to send messages to General Thomas Jordan. They uncovered traitorous correspondence all through her house. One letter was found torn to pieces in the fireplace. Pinkerton pasted it back together. He also found Greenhow's small red diary that listed her couriers and fellow spies. More arrests were made of many notable and respected people—senators, army officers, a dentist, a banker, and a lawyer.

For several months, Greenhow was shown leniency and kept under house arrest. But they soon found out it didn't stop her from spying.

"The lady was discovered on several occasions attempting to send messages to her rebel friends," said Pinkerton. "And finally her removal to the Old Capitol Prison was ordered."

Pinkerton wanted the Confederate spies to face the consequences.

"I sympathize with any and every person who is deprived of liberty," Pinkerton wrote in his report to Brigadier General Andrew Porter, Provost-Marshal. "But it is far better that a few should suffer than that the lives of our best men and bravest soldiers should be sacrificed."

Rebel Rose was held as a prisoner for a year and nine months. She was never tried for treason. Instead, she was shown leniency and exiled to the South.

When Pinkerton's spies were captured behind enemy lines, they wouldn't be so lucky.

Chapter 8
No Way Out

Washington, D.C., February 1862

Pinkerton was worried. Several weeks ago, he'd sent Timothy Webster and Hattie Lawton across enemy lines into Richmond, Virginia—the capital of the Confederacy. But no one had heard from them. Pinkerton was desperate to know if something went wrong, even though he knew Webster was a very capable spy.

"Webster's talent in sustaining a *role* ... amounted to positive genius," said Pinkerton. "And it was this that forced me to admire the man as sincerely as I prized his services."

After Pinkerton set up the Secret Service headquarters in Washington, he sent Webster to Baltimore, where he was to become popular with the secessionists while gathering information on secret plots and movements of traitors. He went undercover as a wealthy gentleman and Southern sympathizer, living at Miller's Hotel, a secessionist hot spot. Pinkerton gave him a pair of fine horses and a carriage, plus plenty of money to spend at saloons where he was to make friends. Always well-mannered and amicable, Webster discussed politics calmly and with conviction.

Although he had some acquaintances in Baltimore from his time spent in Perrymansville during the Baltimore Plot, within a week he was the leader of a clique—looked up to and highly regarded.

But it wasn't always smooth sailing. When Webster made his way back to Washington, D.C., to secretly meet with Pinkerton to give him a verbal report, a man named Bill Zigler saw him talking to Pinkerton. Zigler was the ringleader of a gang of ruffians in Baltimore. Webster always avoided him.

When Webster returned to Baltimore, Zigler called him a spy in front of a crowd in the saloon. Stunned, Webster quickly called him a liar and punched him so hard between the eyes that Zigler was knocked across the room. Zigler stood up and rushed toward him with a knife. But Webster pulled out his revolver.

"Hold your distance, you miserable cur," said Webster. "Or your blood will be upon your own head."

Turning pale, Zigler backed away.

"Coward," said Webster. "If I served you right, I would shoot you down like a dog."

Zigler slinked out of the saloon.

"I cannot conceive what that fellow has against me, that he should try to defame my character by such an accusation," said Webster.

Confederate General John H. Winder.

Everyone agreed. And Webster's cover was safe, for now.

Soon after, Webster managed to infiltrate the covert Knights of Liberty. The secret organization was planning an attack on Washington, D.C., with an army of ten thousand Confederates. Webster believed the numbers were exaggerated, but he saw their arsenal of weapons. He alerted Pinkerton, who in turn had the leaders in the organization arrested, including Webster—that way, no one would know he was a Union spy.

Afterward, Webster went to Richmond, Virginia. Still undercover as a wealthy gentleman, Webster had letters of introduction from his "friends" in Baltimore, allowing him to meet people and infiltrate Richmond. He posed as a Confederate mail courier from Baltimore using the Secret Line, the Confederate communications system.

Brigadier General John Henry Winder was Richmond's head of military police, or provost marshal, who ran counter-intelligence and oversaw the prisoners of war. Webster won over Winder by delivering letters to and from Winder's son, who was an officer in the Union army in Washington. In return, Winder gave Webster a much-needed and highly valued pass that allowed him to travel freely through the Confederate states.

Webster was so good at his job that the Confederate secretary of war, Judah P. Benjamin, made him a special agent. Webster's job as a special agent was to carry the mail from Richmond to Baltimore.

Benjamin had no idea that Webster made a secret stop in Washington, D.C., where the letters were steamed open, the information written down, and the letters carefully resealed before Webster delivered them to the intended person. This led to the arrest of a Confederate spy in the provost marshal's office in Washington, D.C.

✕

"The information he derived was exceedingly valuable," said Pinkerton. "He was able to report very correctly the number and strength around the rebel capital, to estimate the number of troops, and their sources of supplies . . . and his notes of topography of the country were of greatest value."

In January 1862, Webster returned to Richmond, but this time Hattie Lawton went with him, posing as his wife, using the name Sarah Webster. She had also been successful crossing rebel lines. Lawton had infiltrated Southern society, posing as a Southern belle, which allowed her to cultivate friendships with prominent people.

But Pinkerton was worried.

"I heard nothing further from him, directly, and for weeks was utterly ignorant of his movements or conditions," said Pinkerton.

So Pinkerton asked his detectives Pryce Lewis and John Scully to go to Richmond. The mission was straightforward—find out what happened to Webster and Lawton.

But Pryce Lewis refused.

"It would be folly," he told Pinkerton.

Lewis wasn't worried about his ability to find Webster. He was worried someone would recognize him. Lewis had arrested a lot of Southern sympathizers in Washington, D.C., and many of them had been exiled to Richmond.

But Pinkerton was persuasive. He believed his sources were reliable, assuring Lewis that the people he had arrested were not living in Richmond.

Lewis reluctantly changed his mind. He and John Scully, an Irishman who enjoyed knocking back whiskey, would go undercover. Before leaving, Pinkerton gave them a bag of gold coins and outfitted them in new suits so they would look the part of British cotton merchants.

After crossing the Potomac River during a savage storm and nearly drowning, Lewis and Scully arrived in Richmond on February 26. They immediately started looking for Webster by checking all the hotels and asking if he was a guest. It didn't take them long to find him at the Monumental Hotel.

When they entered his room, Webster was in bed. And he was in agony. He was suffering from rheumatism, an extremely painful condition that causes the body's joints and muscles to stiffen. Webster couldn't get out of bed, and Hattie Lawton, who was also in the room, had been busy taking care of him.

Lewis and Scully didn't stay long. They decided to come back later so Webster could get the "mail"—meaning some

Castle Thunder, the Confederate prison where Pinkerton's spies were locked up.

intelligence reports—ready for Lewis and Scully to take back to Pinkerton.

But when they arrived the next day, there was another visitor at Webster's bedside. He introduced himself as Webster's friend, Samuel McCubbin. Although McCubbin was friendly, he stared hard at them, making Lewis's blood run cold. That's because McCubbin was the head of detectives for Confederate general John Winder. McCubbin's job was to arrest spies. Nevertheless, McCubbin was cordial and left shortly after asking Webster about his health.

Pinkerton's operatives carried on with their business and were deep in discussion when there was a knock on the door. George Clackner, a Confederate detective, walked in. Right behind him was Chase Morton—a man Lewis and Scully had guarded after his family was arrested for spying in Washington, D.C. It was a chance encounter. Morton immediately recognized them. With their cover blown, he and Scully were arrested for spying.

✕

Lewis and Scully were taken to Henrico County Jail. For the first two weeks, using a stolen kitchen knife, Lewis sawed, little by little, through the iron bars. Scaling the prison wall, he and ten other prisoners escaped on March 16. Running for their lives, they fled toward the Chickahominy River.

The swampy terrain made it difficult to keep their footing, and they slipped and fell into the icy water. Everyone pushed on, walking to fend off the cold. At dawn, too exhausted to continue, they slept, hidden in the trees. When Lewis woke up, their damp clothes were now frozen stiff. They pushed themselves to keep moving—frozen, hungry, and tired. But the following day, everyone was captured after being spotted on a road to Fredericksburg, twenty miles outside of Richmond. Hordes of people gathered along the streets of Richmond to catch a glimpse of the horse-drawn wagons carrying the "Yankee Jail Breakers."

Lewis, who was now shackled in leg irons, and Scully were transferred to Castle Goodwin prison, a former slave pen. Both were tried for spying and found guilty on April 1, 1862. Their sentence: death by hanging on April 4.

When the verdict was read Lewis wrote, "It turned me to stone, but I did not betray my emotion."

On April 3, the night before their hanging, Scully broke down. He tearfully told Lewis he had sent a message through the priest to Confederate General Winder saying he would confess to spying if he was given a pardon.

The news stunned Lewis. "The ground slipped from under my feet. I felt dizzy and hot. I had to sit down."

At one o'clock in the morning, Lewis was still awake in his cell. He heard a horse-drawn carriage outside. When he looked out his window, he saw Timothy Webster and Hattie Lawton being brought into the prison.

The next morning, at eleven o'clock, while Lewis was waiting to be hanged, the door opened. It was the Catholic priest.

"I have good news for you, Lewis," he said. "President Davis has respited you for two weeks."

But the priest made it clear that it didn't mean Lewis wouldn't hang. "I think you should tell the authorities all you know," he said.

✕

Too weak to get out of bed, Webster's trial for spying was conducted on April 2 at his bedside. Webster was sentenced to die by hanging.

Pinkerton was in the field with McClellan and the army, just south of Richmond, when he learned about the arrests of his operatives. He was reading the Richmond newspaper when he came across the headline: THE CONDEMNED SPIES.

The article, printed on April 5, stated that their executions were to have already taken place. The gallows were built. But Scully's and Lewis's executions were postponed. Then Pinkerton read about Webster's fate:

> *It is intimated, and we believe on good authority, too, that the condemned have made disclosures affecting . . . several persons. Rumor had it yesterday that one of the parties thus implicated was an officer holding a place under the Government. If rumor speaks truth, he will find himself, no doubt, in an uncomfortably hot place.*

"I cannot detail the effect which this announcement produced on me," said Pinkerton. "For a moment I sat almost stupefied, and unable to move. My blood seemed to freeze in my veins—my heart stood still—I was speechless."

Pinkerton hurried to General McClellan and told him the news. They discussed how to get them released.

"All that night I paced the camp, unable to sleep—unable almost to think intelligently," said Pinkerton.

The next morning, Pinkerton sent a telegraph to Captain Milward at Fort Monroe in Hampton, Virginia. Milward was in charge of the flag-of-truce boat for exchanging Confederate prisoners of war for Union prisoners of war. Pinkerton asked him to find out from his sources anything he could about the fate of Lewis, Scully, Webster, and Lawton.

When Milward informed him that Timothy Webster was considered the chief spy, and was sentenced to die, it was a crushing blow to Pinkerton.

Desperate to try and help them, he pleaded with McClellan to send a flag of truce and bargain for their lives. But McClellan was worried that if he did, it would be admitting they were spies, resulting in an immediate execution.

Instead, McClellan sent Pinkerton and Colonel Thomas Key to President Lincoln to ask him to hold a special Cabinet meeting, which Lincoln did. Lincoln authorized Secretary of War Edwin Stanton to send a flag of truce and a dispatch, trying to persuade the Confederacy to reconsider Webster's verdict. Lincoln warned the Confederacy that he would start hanging Confederate spies if they hanged Webster. But they refused to show leniency.

✕

Webster didn't want to be hanged like a murderer. It was considered a disgrace. The day before he was to be executed, Webster asked to speak to Confederate General Winder. He came to Webster's prison cell.

"My fate is sealed," said Webster. "I know that too well—I am to die, and I wish to die like a man. I know there is no hope for mercy, but, sir, I beseech you to permit me to be shot, not be hanged like a common felon—anything but that."

But Winder refused his request.

"I cannot alter the sentence that has been ordered," he said.

✕

On April 29, 1862, a large crowd of people gathered at Camp Lee, a training camp for Confederate soldiers. They were there to witness the first Civil War spy to be executed.

Guards walked Timothy Webster to the gallows. His arms were tied behind his back and his feet were bound. Still weak, his face was pale, but his expression showed no emotion. His coffin was in plain sight.

The cotton rope with the hangman's noose was slipped around his neck. After a prayer was read, a black hood was placed over his head. A signal was given, and the trapdoor under his feet snapped open.

The noose slid over his head, and he slammed down onto the ground. Half-hung, Webster was lying on his back, stunned.

The guards picked him up and carried him back onto the scaffold.

"I suffer a double death," said Webster.

They placed a new rope around his neck and tightened it.

"You will choke me to death this time," said Webster.

At 11:22 a.m., the trapdoor swung open for a second time. One minute later, Timothy Webster was dead.

Chapter 9
The Bloodiest Day

Antietam Creek, Maryland, September 16, 1862

When Pinkerton learned that Timothy Webster was buried in a pauper's grave in Richmond, it tormented him. He tried to have Webster's body sent back north, but Winder refused.

Pinkerton vowed to one day bring Webster's body back home for a proper burial. It was a promise he would keep. But right now, there was only one thing he could do—throw himself into his work to help the Union win the war.

×

Since March, Pinkerton and his Secret Service had been traveling with McClellan on the front lines and assessing the military strength and movements of the Confederate army.

"It was arranged that whenever the army moved I was to go forward with the general," said Pinkerton. "So that I might always be in close communication with him."

Joining Pinkerton on the front lines and helping him with the spy work was his fifteen-year-old son, Billy. Although

Allan Pinkerton, Abraham Lincoln, and Major General John A. McClernand at the Secret Service field headquarters at Antietam during the Civil War.

Allan Pinkerton and his spies. Back row, left to right: H. B. Seybolt, Paul Dennis, an unidentified provost guard, Allan Pinkerton, an unidentified provost guard, George Bangs, an unidentified provost guard, John Babcock, Bob Pinkerton. Front row, left to right: Paul Dennis, D. G. McCaulvey, Billy Pinkerton, Sam Bridgeman. Lying down in front on the left is William B. Watts, chief wagon master, and on the right is Sam Washington, cook.

Pinkerton had wanted Billy to stay in school at Notre Dame, Billy had dropped out to run off and join the Union army. Pinkerton had him transferred to the Secret Service.

Like his father, Billy was determined and relentless, possessing a natural talent for detective work. He had a great memory with an eye for details, never forgetting a face.

Pinkerton put Billy to work as a courier, crossing enemy lines. Sometimes he was disguised in a Confederate uniform. Other times he was disguised as a country boy, wearing tattered clothes and going barefoot. Secret messages were hidden between his toes, which he delivered to Union spies. If he got caught, Billy was instructed to cry like a baby and dig his toes nervously into the ground to destroy the messages.

The information in Pinkerton's reports to McClellan was not just collected by his spies. He also interrogated deserters, prisoners of war, refugees, and runaway slaves. All of this information was vital to McClellan's plan of action, and McClellan wanted Pinkerton to be nearby to provide up-to-date reports.

Confederate general Robert E. Lee was boldly pushing his troops forward onto Union soil. He and his army had successfully defended Richmond, pushing McClellan and his troops back, had scored a victory at the Second Battle of Bull Run, and had captured the Union garrison at Harper's Ferry in Virginia. Now he wanted to invade Maryland, make it a part of the Confederacy, and move into Pennsylvania.

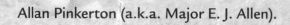
Allan Pinkerton (a.k.a. Major E. J. Allen).

McClellan and his army were on the defensive, trying to protect Maryland and take action against the invasion. In preparing his strategy, McClellan's biggest worry was the number of enemy troops. He didn't want to be outnumbered. To compensate, McClellan knowingly used inflated numbers so he could request more troops.

In a report to McClellan, Pinkerton wrote:

> *That estimate was founded upon all information then in my possession, derived from my own operatives, deserters from the Rebel service, "Contrabands" [slaves] . . . and was made large, as intimated to you at the time, so as to be sure and cover the entire number of the Enemy that our army was to meet.*

For the past two days, McClellan had been positioning his soldiers to drive Lee's troops out of Maryland. The impending battle was going to be a turning point. In a report dated September 11, McClellan wrote:

> *. . . If we defeat the army arrayed before us, the rebellion is crushed. For I do not believe they can organize another army. But if we should be so unfortunate as to meet with defeat, our country is at their mercy.*

On September 15, Lincoln sent a telegram to McClellan. It read:

God bless you and all with you. Destroy the rebel army if possible.

On the morning of September 16, Pinkerton went on a reconnoitering mission with General McClellan's cavalry. Pinkerton wanted to see the position of the Confederate troops with his own eyes. As he rode his horse, scanning the surrounding area, Pinkerton noticed that some of the enemy troops had changed the position of their batteries.

When Pinkerton and the cavalry slowed down to cross the stream, a hailstorm of exploding bullets suddenly erupted from a hidden Confederate battery up on a hill. While the Confederate soldiers opened fire, Pinkerton and the other men scrambled to take cover. But a bullet tore into Pinkerton's horse. They fell into the water. His horse was dead. Stunned, Pinkerton managed to climb up onto the back of a cavalry officer's horse, and they took cover in the nearby woods.

"Several of the men who accompanied me were seriously wounded," said Pinkerton. "And I narrowly escaped with my life."

That was just a preview of the carnage to come.

✕

On the following day, McClellan's plan was to attack the Confederate soldiers on the left, then attack the Confederate soldiers on the right. And, with any soldiers he had left, he would finally attack the center.

At daybreak, more than one thousand Union troops were slowly making their way through a cornfield. The rough stalks hid them from the enemy. But at the same time, they couldn't see the Confederate soldiers who were only two hundred yards in front of them, lying in wait with their guns pointed and ready to fire.

As soon as the Union soldiers emerged from the cornfield, the Confederates blasted their guns. Chaos erupted—smoke, bullets, screams, and blood. Union and Confederate soldiers dropped to the ground, dead or wounded.

More Confederates streamed out of the surrounding woods and into the cornfield, coming face-to-face with more Union soldiers called in from reserve. Fierce fighting ensued, leaving ten thousand soldiers dead or wounded. And that was just the beginning.

The next twelve hours led to a savage bloodbath. On average, there was a casualty every two seconds. By the end of the day, twenty-three thousand soldiers were dead or wounded. It was the bloodiest one-day battle in American history.

"The dead are strewn so thickly that as you ride over it you cannot guide your horse's steps too carefully. Pale and bloody faces are everywhere upturned. They are sad and terrible, but there is nothing which makes one's heart beat so quickly as the imploring look of sorely wounded men who beckon wearily for help which you cannot stay to give," George Smalley reported in the *New-York Tribune*.

Dead Confederate soldiers in the "Sunken Road"
after the bloodiest one-day battle in US history.

At sunset, the Union army and the Confederate army were both holding their positions. It was a tactical draw. McClellan knew that Lincoln wanted him to continue the attack and destroy the rebels. But he hesitated.

Even though he'd received thousands of additional troops, McClellan was still worried he was outnumbered by the Confederates. He believed Lee had one hundred thousand troops, insisting that the capture of Harper's Ferry allowed for an additional forty thousand Confederate troops to fight in Antietam. In reality, McClellan had eighty-seven thousand troops, nearly double that of the Confederates. McClellan wrote in his report:

Whether to renew the attack on the 18th or to defer, even with the risk of the enemy's retirement, was the question before me.

After a night of anxious deliberation, and a full and careful survey of the situation and condition of our army, the strength and position of the enemy, I concluded that the success of an attack on the 18th was not certain. I am aware of the fact that under ordinary circumstances a general is expected to risk a battle if he has a reasonable prospect of success . . . At that moment—Virginia lost, Washington menaced, Maryland invaded—the national cause could afford no risks of defeat. One battle lost and almost all would have been lost. Lee's army might then have marched, as it pleased, on Washington, Baltimore, Philadelphia, or New York.

McClellan's cautious decision was going to cost him. The next day, September 18, Confederate General Lee expected another attack. When it didn't happen, he quickly withdrew his troops.

Although the Battle of Antietam was over, it had one more casualty. It ended General McClellan's military career.

McClellan and Pinkerton were both severely criticized for overestimating the number of enemy troops. McClellan wrote in a paper that additions were "made for the sake of safety, to the known quantities: which may have created the impression that the force of the enemy in front of Washington was exaggerated."

Lincoln was frustrated with McClellan's repeated refusal to go after the enemy. McClellan had failed to destroy Lee's army and end the Civil War. On November 5, 1862, Lincoln fired McClellan, replacing him with General Ambrose Burnside.

Despite all the criticism surrounding McClellan, Pinkerton remained steadfast and true to him.

"No general in this country, or in any other, was more universally beloved and admired by his troops," said Pinkerton. "And no commander ever returned that affection with more warmth than did McClellan."

Pinkerton didn't want to work with General Burnside. He didn't have confidence in him. The feeling was mutual.

In protest to McClellan's firing, Pinkerton resigned.

"Upon the removal of General McClellan, I declined to act any further in the capacity in which I had previously served, although strongly urged to do so by both President Lincoln and the secretary of war, Edwin M. Stanton," said Pinkerton.

✕

After severing his ties with the Secret Service and turning his back on espionage, Pinkerton returned to being a detective, working for the War Department in Washington, D.C. He was kept busy chasing down numerous thieves who were robbing the government. Both of his sons, Billy and Bob, now worked with him.

Although Pinkerton had hoped that his younger son, Bob, would stay in school and become a doctor or lawyer, in 1864, sixteen-year-old Bob ran away from Notre Dame and forcefully told his father that he was going to be a detective. Pinkerton conceded, and was training both sons to take part in the dangerous and oftentimes violent family business.

Throughout the war, Pinkerton's National Detective Agency in Chicago remained open—thanks, in a large part, to George Bangs. He worked tirelessly trying to keep up with the work, and nearly ruined his health in doing so.

Two of Pinkerton's spies who did not return to work for the agency were John Scully and Pryce Lewis. Scully confessed to the Confederates, and by giving up Webster as a spy, he saved their lives. They were released from prison two weeks after the Battle of Antietam. But they were also considered informers, especially by Pinkerton, who looked at it as an unforgivable betrayal.

Throughout Lewis's life, he denied confessing to the Confederates. He steadfastly maintained that Scully gave up Webster as a spy. But Pinkerton didn't believe him—and that would haunt Lewis for the rest of his life.

Pinkerton's spy Hattie Lawton was released from prison in January 1863. Her whereabouts after being set free remain a mystery.

✕

On April 9, 1865, the Civil War officially ended when Confederate general Robert E. Lee surrendered. On the night of April 14, Abraham Lincoln went to watch a play at Ford's Theatre in Washington, D.C. At Lincoln's request, his usual bodyguard, Ward Lamon, was traveling to Richmond. So John Parker, a local police officer, was hired to stand guard at the entrance of the presidential box and protect Lincoln during the entire performance.

But after the curtain went up and the play began, Parker left his post. Just after ten o'clock, while Parker was having a drink in the Star Saloon next door, John Wilkes Booth shot Abraham Lincoln in the head. By morning, Lincoln was dead.

Pinkerton, who was in New Orleans investigating cotton thieves, woke up to the news on April 19, 1865. He wept.

Then Pinkerton sent a telegram to the War Department in Washington, D.C., offering his services to hunt down the killer.

"How I regret that I had not been near him previous to the fatal act. I might have had the means to arrest it," Pinkerton wrote in the telegram.

But by the time he received a reply from Secretary of War Edwin Stanton, Lincoln's killer, John Wilkes Booth, was already dead.

✕

On the same day that Pinkerton found out about the assassination of President Lincoln, the mirrors and chandeliers in the White House were already covered with black cloth. His funeral procession had begun.

Two days later, on April 21, the murdered president was loaded onto a train. His casket traveled nearly the same route that he took when he was on his way to his first inauguration as the president-elect—Baltimore, Philadelphia, and Harrisburg—180 cities in all. At each stop his casket was unloaded, so that the thousands and thousands of mourners in each city could pay their last respects. His final stop was Springfield, Illinois, his hometown, where he was laid to rest.

Chapter 10
Reign of Terror

Seymour, Indiana, October 6, 1866

It was 6:30 p.m. on Saturday when the train whistle howled and the metal wheels clanked, slowly picking up speed and chugging steadily over the tracks from the depot in Seymour, Indiana. For most people on the train—made up of an engine, tender, baggage, passenger coach, and Adams Express car—they couldn't get out of town fast enough.

Travelers were warned to stay away from Seymour—a town where robberies and murders were so commonplace it was called a "carnival of crime." And if they had the misfortune of spending the night at a local hotel, the Rader House, the headquarters for a notorious gang of bandits, they were guaranteed to wake up penniless—if they woke up at all.

As the train flew down the tracks, three men in the passenger car stood up. No one could easily recognize them because they had masks covering their faces. They quickly made their way to the Adams Express car, the railroad car

where cash, gold, and bonds were locked up in safes. No one stopped them because they had guns in their hands.

The masked men forced open the door to the Adams Express car. Inside they found the Adams Express messenger, the person in charge of safely delivering the money. Holding a pistol to his head, they threatened to kill him. He handed the keys to the masked men, who unlocked the safe.

Inside they found $15,000 in gold coin. And there was an even bigger safe onboard, which would bring the total up to $45,000. But try as they might, the masked men couldn't open it. When the messenger said he couldn't open it, either, they beat him up, and then they rolled the unopened safe to the door.

One of the masked men rang a bell, signaling the engineer to stop the train. The train slammed on its brakes, and as the train slowed down, the masked men rolled the safe out the door and jumped off.

"All right!" one of the masked men yelled to the engineer.

And when the train picked up speed, rumbling down the tracks and out of sight, the three men took off their masks. The Reno Brothers Gang had successfully pulled off a new kind of crime—the moving train robbery.

But the brothers ran into some unexpected trouble. First, the safe couldn't be cracked, so they were forced to abandon it. Second, Adams Express hired Allan Pinkerton.

After the Civil War, the railroad lines rapidly expanded across the entire country. Powerful steam locomotives hurtled down newly laid railroad tracks, linking fast-growing

Frank Reno of the infamous Reno Gang—the first organized band of outlaws.

cities to isolated and lawless frontier towns. Compared to the horse-drawn stagecoach, which also carried mail, money, and passengers at a top speed of nine miles per hour, the train could now travel five hundred miles in one day at half the cost. It was the latest and greatest mode of transportation. But it was still a target for crime. This was good news for Pinkerton's National Detective Agency.

Despite the economic depression that followed the Civil War, the business of catching criminals was booming. To keep up, Pinkerton not only had a detective agency in Chicago but he also opened an office in New York City. Long-time detective and friend George Bangs had proven to be such a good business administrator that Pinkerton put him in charge of the New York office. Pinkerton was also planning to open another office in Philadelphia. But first, he had to catch the Reno Brothers Gang.

It wasn't going to be easy. After Pinkerton visited Seymour, Indiana, he knew this wasn't just a straightforward train robbery. The Reno Gang used threats, bribes, and extreme violence to control the citizens and public officials of Seymour and the surrounding towns. No one was going to speak out against the Reno Brothers—not if they valued their property or their lives.

✕

Soon after Pinkerton's visit to Seymour, a new saloon opened in town. And even though the Rader House was the Reno

Brothers Gang's headquarters, the new saloon was quickly a favorite hangout. The saloonkeeper, Dick Winscott, who said he was hiding out in Seymour after getting in some hot water back east, served plenty of drinks to the Reno brothers and their gang.

John Reno, the oldest brother, was the leader of the gang. Frank, the second-oldest brother, was the second-in-command. Younger brothers Simeon and William were also in the gang. Only one brother didn't join in—"Honest Clint." Their sister, Laura, also wasn't a member. But she was fiercely loyal to her brothers, ready to seek vengeance if anyone wronged them. Gang members outside of the family included counterfeiters, thieves, safecrackers, and assassins.

But there was one regular at Dick Winscott's saloon who wasn't part of the Reno Brothers Gang. Even so, he could always be found sitting at the table playing poker with the Reno Brothers. Like Winscott, he was new to town. He was a tall man with a ruddy complexion and muttonchop whiskers. He went by the name Phil Oates and said he was a gambler, traveling from town to town.

It was a known fact that the Reno Brothers loved to gamble. They always had plenty of money and spent it freely. But the townsfolk knew that the wads of cash they carried weren't winnings from gambling—no one was that lucky.

The townsfolk suspected the Reno Brothers were the culprits in a rash of robberies—homes, business, and post offices. But no one was going to say anything. They knew better.

When one neighbor made the mistake of openly talking in public about his suspicions, he soon found himself with a barn burned to the ground and his horses dead. But he was fortunate.

In 1865, when gang member Grant Wilson was arrested for one of their many robberies, he snitched on Frank. But Wilson never testified against him. He was murdered before the trial. Frank got off scot-free. And everyone quickly learned not to breathe a word against the Reno Brothers.

And if anyone made the mistake of trying to move in on their turf, the Reno Brothers would beat them up, steal their loot, and tip off the sheriff to have them arrested.

But the Reno Brothers were often in a jovial mood after downing some liquor and winning at cards at Winscott's saloon. And as the nights wore on into the wee hours of the morning, Winscott and Oates learned plenty about the Reno Brothers. And afterward, they would take pen to paper and write it all down, then send it to their employer, Allan Pinkerton.

✕

On November 17, 1867, John Reno and some gang members robbed $22,065 from the county treasury in Daviess County, Missouri, not far from the city of Gallatin. Dick Winscott confirmed that the Reno Brothers were to blame. Even so, he told Pinkerton it was a bad idea for him to come into Seymour and try to arrest any of the Reno Brothers. Not unless he

John and Frank Reno. A saloon keeper talked John and Frank into having this photo taken, which became part of Pinkerton's Rogues' Gallery.

wanted a shootout. But Pinkerton came up with a plan, and if it was timed just right, no one would have a chance to shoot.

$$\times$$

On December 4, 1867, John Reno was standing on the train platform in Seymour talking to his friend Dick Winscott. There was a large group gathered; most were waiting for the train to bring the mail. John was waiting for a friend.

The express train was supposed to arrive any minute. But just before its scheduled arrival time, a special train, with only the locomotive and one car attached, pulled in. John didn't think anything of it—until Pinkerton and his six brawniest detectives got off the train and quickly surrounded him.

Before John had time to pull out his revolver, his hands were cuffed. Kicking and screaming, John was loaded onto the train. When the Reno Gang members heard the news, they quickly hopped on their horses and rode after the train. But they were too late.

Pinkerton's plan had worked. For the past two days, he and the sheriff of Daviess County had been standing by in Cincinnati with an arrest warrant and the special train ready to go—once they received the telegram from Winscott letting them know the time John would be at the depot.

John Reno was tried and convicted for robbing the Daviess County treasury. He was transferred to Missouri's state prison on January 18, 1868. He was sentenced to twenty-five years' hard labor.

$$\times$$

Pinkerton thought that once the leader of the Reno Gang was behind bars, the gang would fall apart. Instead, Frank Reno became the leader, and there was no slowing them down. The gang robbed trains, county treasuries, and post offices in Indiana, Missouri, and Iowa.

Soon after John Reno was sent to jail, Frank and his gang stole $14,000 from the Harrison County Treasury in Magnolia, Iowa. For the small frontier settlement it was a catastrophe.

Billy Pinkerton (middle) with railroad special agents Pat Connell (left) and Sam Finley. Billy chased down the Reno Brothers and the James-Younger Gang, to name a few.

Pinkerton sent his son Billy to investigate. When Billy arrived at the scene of the robbery, he learned the thieves made their getaway using a handcar, heading down the railroad tracks in the direction of Council Bluffs, Iowa. At Council Bluffs, Billy quickly discovered a saloon run by a former resident of Seymour.

For the next two days, Billy kept a close watch on the saloon, noticing the same tall man talked to the saloon-keeper for extended periods of time. It turned out that the man was Michael Rogers, a wealthy and respected citizen in Council Bluffs. This bit of information didn't stop Billy's investigation.

Like his father, Billy was persistent. He knew firsthand that detective work involved painstaking attention to details, a good memory, and some luck.

So Billy staked out Rogers's house. And on the fourth day, he saw Rogers leave with three strangers, one who looked suspiciously like Frank Reno. He watched them get on a train and leave. But he didn't follow them. He knew they'd come back. So he waited.

The following morning, he saw Rogers and the three men come back to Rogers's house. But now they were disheveled and covered in mud. Later that morning, Billy heard the news that in Glenwood, about thirty miles away, the county treasurer had been robbed. The thieves had escaped on a handcar, which was found not far from the Council Bluffs train station.

When Billy went to the local authorities for a search warrant, they laughed. They couldn't believe that Rogers was a thief.

Nevertheless, Billy placed an armed guard at the front and back doors of Rogers's home and knocked on the door. When Rogers answered, he was clearly unhappy to have a visitor. Billy ignored his hostility, asking him who he had in the house.

"Nobody but my family," said Rogers.

"We'll see about that," said Billy.

He and the guards started to search the house. Billy went into the kitchen and came upon the strangers. They were just about to sit down and have breakfast. He recognized Frank Reno from a photo. Two other Reno Gang members were with him, Albert Perkins and Miles Ogle—Ogle was well on his way to becoming a notorious counterfeiter.

While Billy and the guards handcuffed them, he smelled smoke and noticed a sudden blaze coming from the kitchen stove. He pulled off the lid and saw bundles of money on top of the hot coals. He reached in and grabbed them. Luckily, the bills had been so tightly wrapped that only the outer bills were singed. The banknotes were identified as the stolen money from the Glenwood safe.

Billy hauled Frank Reno and his gang to the Glenwood jail where they would wait for a trial. But the next morning, on April 1, when the sheriff went into the jail, their cells were empty. There was a big hole where they had bashed in the brick wall. Right above the hole was a message written on the wall. It said, "April Fool."

✕

A huge reward was offered for the capture of the Reno Brothers Gang. But for the next couple of months they laid low—until May 22, 1868, when Frank Reno and his gang robbed the Adams Express car in Marshfield, Indiana.

Forcing their way into the Adams Express car, they savagely beat the Adams Express messenger, throwing him off the moving train and fatally injuring him. Learning from their mistakes, they expertly broke open the iron safes and found nearly $100,000 in gold, banknotes, and bonds. It was their biggest robbery to date.

✕

With the loot in hand, they rode their horses to Seymour, stopping at the Rader House, the Reno Brothers' headquarters. After dividing the loot, they split up, leaving town to go into hiding. They knew once Pinkerton heard the news, he'd be hot on their trail.

"I'm the worst enemy they've got in the world, and they know it," said Pinkerton. "I'm here to bring justice to the worst gang of scoundrels in the country. It's going to be a hard fight, but I'll win."

Chapter 11
Wanted Dead or Alive

Brownstown, Indiana, July 10, 1868

With the Reno Brothers Gang on the run from the law, the town of Seymour and the surrounding area grew quiet, almost peaceful. It wouldn't last for long.

Early in the morning on July 10, the eastbound Ohio & Mississippi Valley train made an unscheduled stop at the Brownstown depot, not far from Seymour. James Flanders, the engineer, stepped down. While he looked busy inspecting the train's engine, three bandits surrounded him with loaded revolvers.

The Reno Gang—John Moore, Henry Jerrell, Frank Sparks, Volney Elliott, Charlie Roseberry, and Theodore Clifton—was back. The engineer surrendered without a fight. That was part of the plan. The robbery was an inside job. Flanders was to be paid off later when they divided the loot.

The Reno Gang quickly uncoupled the express car from the rest of the train before hopping on. As the engine and express car headed down the tracks, they pushed the man in charge of stoking the fire out the door. Then they shot their pistols into the air, signaling victory. Or so they thought.

After a few miles, they stopped the train in a secluded spot and rushed toward the express car. When the door was thrown open, six Pinkerton detectives greeted them with blasting guns—the Reno Gang had been double-crossed. Flanders, the train's engineer, never planned on helping them rob the train. Instead, he told the railroad officials about their plans.

Quick on the draw, the bandits fired back. But the Pinks had better aim. Gang member John Moore was shot in his side, and Frank Sparks's finger was shot clean off his hand. Even so, the bandits kept firing. Until their most audacious member, Volney Elliott, was shot in the shoulder and fell to the ground. That's when the rest of the gang took off running for their lives.

✕

The search was on, and two days later, gang members Charlie Roseberry and Theodore Clifton were found hiding in a dense thicket. They were put in jail with Volney Elliott in Seymour for safekeeping.

On the night of July 20, the three prisoners were escorted into a train at the Seymour depot. They were heading to Brownstown, the scene of their crime. Roseberry, Clifton, and Elliott were scheduled to appear at their preliminary hearing. After two miles down the track, a man was spotted waving a glowing lantern. The train came to a sudden stop.

Within seconds, a large group of men, all wearing scarlet masks, jumped on board the train. The masked men overpowered the guards, grabbed the prisoners, and hurried away up a narrow lane. The prisoners were rescued. Or so it seemed. Then they saw the beech tree with the ropes dangling from a limb.

The masked men were members of the newly formed Vigilance Committe of Southern Indiana. Typical for the times, citizens banded together, taking the law into their own hands and delivering swift, rough justice. This was especially common in the wild frontier, where law and order were hard to come by, and, as a result, there were hundreds of vigilante groups. Law-abiding citizens generally viewed vigilantes as heroes who filled a gap in weak or nonexistent law enforcement. So tonight, the Vigilance Committee of Southern Indiana was going to make sure the Reno Brothers Gang paid for their crimes.

When the gang members were asked to confess, Roseberry didn't say a word. Clifton fell to his knees. He swore his innocence and asked them to spare his life. But Elliott was defiant.

"Confess, hell; I'd tell you nothing," he said. "You've got me here, a thousand of you, now do your worst."

The nooses were tightened around each one of their

necks. The barrels they were standing on were kicked away. Instantly, they were hanging by their necks, their bodies flailing until finally limp.

✕

The following day, fugitives John Moore, Henry Jerrell, and Frank Sparks were captured in Coles County, where they'd been working as farmhands, under assumed names. The prisoners were to be taken to Brownstown on the night of July 25, but Pinkerton was worried they'd be lynched, too. So he hid the handcuffed and shackled prisoners in a wagon protected by six heavily armed Pinkerton guards.

The wagon bumped along, following the line of the railroad tracks. It made its way past the spot where the other three gang members had been ambushed and crossed the tracks. It passed the beech tree, crossed a small bridge, and turned down a narrow lane. All was well.

Until a large group of about seventy-five men wearing scarlet masks quietly came out of the darkness, rushed the wagon, and overpowered the Pinkerton guards.

John Moore, Henry Jerrell, and Frank Sparks were taken to the same beech tree. Nooses were tightened around their necks. The barrels under their feet were kicked away, and they were swinging from the beech tree, hanged by their necks. The area was soon dubbed Hangman's Crossing.

The Vigilance Committee issued a proclamation, "Should one of our committee be harmed, or a dollar's worth of

WANTED
DEAD OR ALIVE
Contact: Pinkerton's
Detective Agency
FRANKLIN "FRANK" RENO
$5,000 REWARD
NOTORIOUS ROBBER
OF TRAINS AND BANKS

property of any honest man be destroyed, by persons unknown, we will *swing [them] by the neck*, until they be dead, every thieving character we can lay our hands on. This applies not only to Seymour, but along the line of the two roads, and wherever our organization exists. Law and order must prevail."

✕

In the meantime, Pinkerton detectives tracked down and arrested William and Simeon Reno. They'd been hiding in Lexington, Indiana, where they loved to gamble. Fearing the Vigilance Committee would hang her brothers, Laura Reno begged the governor of Indiana to protect them. So William and Simeon were sent to New Albany, Indiana, to await their trial. The jail in New Albany was made of stone—the strongest and sturdiest in all of Indiana.

In August, Pinkerton learned from one of his operatives in Windsor, Canada, a tough town across the river from Detroit where American outlaws were known to hide out, that Frank Reno was holed up there. Pinkerton led the raid at the gang's hideout. Frank was arrested along with three of his gang members—Albert Perkins, safecracker Charlie Anderson, and once-respected Council Bluffs citizen Michael Rogers.

Once Pinkerton had them in his custody, he was faced with the problem of extradition, or bringing them back, to America. The Canadian government didn't want to extradite the gang members if they were going to be lynched. And they let Michael Rogers go free since he claimed it was a case of mistaken identity.

At the time, Rogers was using an alias. Proof of his identity couldn't be furnished to the court—there weren't any photos of him, and fingerprinting didn't exist at the time. Once Rogers was released, he fled the country, crossing the border back into the United States.

For the time being, Pinkerton was going to have to wait for the paperwork and for the Canadian government to give permission to bring back Frank Reno, Albert Perkins, and Charlie Anderson. Even though it would take months, Pinkerton wasn't going to give up. He could wait it out. In the meantime he went back to Chicago.

But the next time Pinkerton returned to bring Frank Reno and Charlie Anderson back, he discovered they weren't about to go down without a fight. In fact, they were willing to do whatever was necessary to stop Pinkerton. Even murder him.

X

On October 15, Pinkerton found himself in a horse-drawn carriage, traveling toward Windsor. He was going to catch the ferry and cross the river to Detroit.

Even though Pinkerton still couldn't bring Reno and Anderson back to the United States, he had been visiting the neighboring town of Sandwich, where Reno and Anderson were jailed. That morning, it was discovered that they had tried to dig their way out of prison. But a fellow prisoner squealed, and they were promptly placed in iron shackles.

As the carriage jostled along the road, Pinkerton spoke to the two other passengers. He didn't know an assassin was following him—until the man rode up alongside the carriage, looked in, and reached for his revolver, pointing it at Pinkerton.

"Look out!" cried a passenger.

Before the gunman had time to fire, the carriage driver sped away.

$$\times$$

Without delay, Pinkerton boarded the next ferry out of town. The journey across the river was uneventful. Until he stepped off the ferryboat and onto the dock.

That's when Pinkerton stumbled. When he righted himself, there was a revolver pointed at his head. The assassin pulled the trigger. But the gun didn't fire.

Pinkerton quickly grabbed the gun with one hand and the throat of the gunman with his other hand. He called out for assistance and held the assassin until the police arrived.

It turned out that the Reno Brothers and Sam Felker, a detective who was working for them, had hired the assassin.

"This diabolical attempt to assassinate Pinkerton has created quite an excitement here, and all law-abiding citizens are thankful that the designs of the scoundrel and his employers have been frustrated," the *Sacramento Daily Union* newspaper reported.

As for Pinkerton, he wasn't going to let two assassination attempts stop him. This wasn't the first time someone had tried to murder him. It was the third.

The very first time someone tried was in 1853, sixteen years ago. It was near midnight, and Pinkerton was walking down the street, on his way home, when an assassin fired his gun at Pinkerton's back. Pinkerton, who had been walking with his left arm swung up behind his back, felt two bullets tear into his forearm. The bullets were shot at such close range that Pinkerton's coat caught on fire. Despite the bullet wound in his left arm, Pinkerton was back at work the next day.

"When my time has come to die, I will die," said Pinkerton. "Until then, these fellows waste their time shooting at me."

✕

About two weeks after the latest assassination attempt, in late October, Frank Reno and Charlie Anderson were extradited. Handcuffed and in iron shackles, Pinkerton took the prisoners aboard a tugboat that he had chartered. It would bypass Detroit and take them to Cleveland. It was a sunny day and the waters were calm. It should've been a smooth ride.

After twenty miles, a large steamer's propeller cut into the tugboat's bow, sinking it. The prisoners were sinking from the weight of the iron shackles and handcuffs. Pinkerton and his men held the outlaws' heads above water. The steamer that sank them, rescued them, pulling everyone on board and taking them to Detroit.

It hadn't been easy, but Pinkerton, who was sick from exhaustion, finally delivered Frank Reno and Charlie Anderson to the New Albany jail in southern Indiana. They joined William and Simeon Reno. Before leaving, Pinkerton inspected the jail. He didn't think the jail was sturdy enough to fend off a lynch mob. He advised the sheriff, Thomas Fullenlove, to secretly transfer the prisoners to a jail in Indianapolis. The sheriff ignored the warning.

✕

On December 12, 1868, sometime after two o'clock in the morning, Sheriff Fullenlove was awakened by a noise outside. The sheriff, who lived at the New Albany jail, got out of bed and, wearing only his underwear and shirt, went across the hall to his office door.

On the other side of the office door stood a large group of well-dressed men wearing red flannel masks. Each masked man carried a heavy club, one or more revolvers, and a slingshot. They had captured the night guards, dragged them to the office, and tied them up.

The masked men were shouting, demanding the keys to the jail. Sheriff Fullenlove ran down the basement steps and slid out a window.

But more masked men were waiting outside. Shots rang out, and a bullet tore into Fullenlove's arm, hitting the bone. Several men grabbed him and gave him a vicious pistol whipping.

Bloody and barely conscious, Fullenlove was carried back inside the jail, where he was guarded. The mob searched everywhere and found the keys. They hurried to the cell room, tied up the guard, and started a new search. This time they were looking for the Reno Gang—Frank, Simeon, and William Reno, plus Charlie Anderson.

Ignoring the Reno Gang's pleas for mercy, the masked men grabbed the prisoners from their jail cells, tied a rope around each of their necks, and hanged them from rafters.

The Reno Gang was dead. And the men in scarlet masks left.

✕

When the hanged men were found and the news spread, Pinkerton was called to the governor's office in Indianapolis for a meeting to discuss the lynchings. Pinkerton didn't have a problem with vigilantism. He viewed it as "fighting fire with fire." When it came to catching criminals, he always upheld the belief that the ends justified the means. Nevertheless, right after the meeting, warnings were published that no one was to take the law into their own hands and that the vigilantes would be found and punished.

But it was an empty threat. Law enforcement officials

were relieved that the Reno Brothers Gang's reign had ended. No one was ever charged or convicted for the murders.

"Retribution is not always swift, but it is always sure," the *Seymour Democrat* newspaper in Seymour, Indiana, stated. "Right or wrong, the Renos met a fearful doom. The New Albany tragedy will give our legislators something to think about. . . . The people will assume their delegated powers if those powers are misused. Give us better criminal code, or the Vigilantes, like a nightmare, will haunt all lawyers and judges for all time to come."

However, the Canadian government was outraged. The *Montreal Herald* newspaper stated, "The American government was strictly responsible for the safety of these men and should be strictly held to account. Extradition must cease if men are sent over the border to be torn to pieces by unauthorized rabble."

Secretary of State William Seward issued an apology on behalf of the United States.

The demise of the Reno Brothers Gang brought an end to the reign of terror in Seymour, Indiana. Even so, their gruesome fate didn't deter other gangs of outlaws from breaking the law.

In fact, the leader of a gang of outlaws in Missouri would soon prove to be not only good at robbing trains but even better at not getting caught. And for the first time in his career as a detective, Pinkerton would be cast as the villain.

Chapter 12
The James-Younger Gang

Corydon, Iowa, June 3, 1871

Everyone knew in the small town of Corydon, Iowa, that it was a big day. They just didn't realize how big.

Nearly all of the townsfolk were attending an open-air meeting on the outskirts of Corydon. They were going to discuss a new railroad line that would run through town. And, to top it off, well-known political activist and Methodist minister Henry Clay Dean was going to speak. No one wanted to miss that.

But Henry Clay Dean's appearance at the town meeting wasn't the only big deal that day—especially for the Ocobock brothers. They had just opened a new bank in Corydon, and business was good. The county treasurer had just made a large deposit after all the taxes had been collected.

So while Henry Clay Dean was giving his speech, sometime after twelve o'clock, Mr. Ocobock stayed at his bank and kept it open for business. But business was slow. That is, until two men came in and pointed their guns at his head, demanding that he open the safe.

Alone, with no one to help him, Mr. Ocobock opened it. The robbers grabbed $6,000 and stuffed it into a saddle bag. Without firing a shot, they ran outside to their horses and took off, riding toward the Missouri River.

As they passed by the town meeting, they fired their guns and shook the bag of money overhead, shouting gleefully, "The Corydon bank has just been robbed!" To add insult to injury, they yelled that the people had "better get back to town and start a new bank quick." The robbers let out a cheer for Lincoln's assassin, John Wilkes Booth, and cursed the "damn Yanks for cowards" before they galloped out of sight.

With the bank's safe now empty, there was only one thing for the Ocobock brothers to do. They hired Pinkerton's National Detective Agency.

$$\times$$

When the Ocobock brothers called in the Pinks, Allan Pinkerton was in no shape to hunt down the outlaws.

For the past few years, Allan Pinkerton had suffered from overwhelming grief from deep personal loss. In January 1868, Pinkerton kept vigil at Kate Warne's bedside as she lay dying from a battle with a long illness. In September 1868, his brother, Robert, also died.

Pinkerton's anguish combined with his unrelenting drive

to constantly work took a heavy toll on his overall health. Despite coming down with a severe cold after nearly drowning while bringing back Frank Reno and Charlie Anderson, Pinkerton refused to slow down. Until he had no choice.

In 1869, Pinkerton was in his office dictating a letter to his secretary when he was struck by an excruciating headache. Seconds later he collapsed. Pinkerton had suffered a massive stroke. At fifty years old, Pinkerton was paralyzed and unable to talk. The news from his doctors was grim. He would never talk or walk again. But the doctors didn't factor in Pinkerton's fierce determination.

Robert Pinkerton (left) and William Pinkerton (right).

Pinkerton's two sons took over the detective agency while Pinkerton set out to prove his doctors wrong. The agency kept Allan's dire condition a secret—to protect his privacy, reputation, and business. So Pinkerton's youngest son, Bob, was sent out to investigate the robbery at the Ocobock brothers' bank.

Tall, broad-shouldered, with a friendly smile and gracious manner, twenty-four-year-old Bob arrived in Corydon, Iowa, where he and the townsfolk saddled up their horses. Together, they tracked the steps of the robbers all the way to Missouri—the "Outlaw State." At this point, the townsfolk ended their search, but, like his father, Bob was hardworking and relentless in his pursuit. He continued the investigation on his own. The trail led him over a hundred miles from Corydon to the border of Clay County, Missouri.

For several days, Bob tried interviewing the people in Clay County, but most of them were tight-lipped on the matter. Even so, he gathered enough information about the history of an avenging gang of bandits who lived there. This information led him to a farmhouse belonging to long-time resident Zerelda Samuel—also known as the mother of Jesse James.

✕

Hard-bitten and tough-as-nails, Jesse's mother was once described by a Union soldier as "one of the worst women in

Seventeen-year-old Jesse James, a guerilla fighter.

this state [Missouri]." The thrice-married Zerelda Samuel was born into a wealthy, slave-owning family and was married to Reuben Samuel, a timid country doctor who was stuck firmly under her thumb. She had a total of seven children—Frank, Jesse, and Susan James, plus Sarah, John, Fannie, and Archie Samuel.

Like most of her neighbors in Clay County, Missouri, Zerelda was a die-hard Southern sympathizer. And she instilled her beliefs in her children.

When the Civil War broke out, her oldest son, eighteen-year-old Frank, joined the Missouri bushwhackers, a group of guerrilla fighters, led by the ferocious Border Ruffian William Quantrill.

Wanted for murder and stealing horses, former school-teacher William Quantrill moved to Kansas in the 1850s at a time when deep-seated hatred between abolitionists and pro-slavery factions was raging, especially along the border between Kansas and Missouri. These already warring sides were killing each other over whether Kansas would be admitted to the Union as a free state or slave state in what is known as the Bleeding of Kansas.

At the outbreak of the Civil War, Quantrill trained a group of men in guerrilla warfare—ambushes, raids, and hit-and-run tactics—and targeted Union soldiers and sympathizers along the Kansas-Missouri border. The James boys would later use these same guerrilla tactics to rob banks and trains.

Former schoolteacher William Quantrill was wanted
for murder and stealing horses before becoming the
guerilla leader of Quantrill's Raiders.

It was while fighting with Quantrill's Raiders that Frank
would become fast friends with future fellow outlaw Cole
Younger.

Cole Younger was still a teenager when he joined
Quantrill's Raiders after antislavery guerrillas burned down
the Youngers' stables and store, stole their horses, murdered
his father, and charged Cole with treason. He was sentenced
to die but averted death by escaping.

Primed for vengeance, Cole Younger found his way to
Quantrill's Raiders. His high-spirited younger brother, Jim,
soon followed.

Sixteen-year-old Jesse James joined Quantrill's Raiders in
1864 after a group of Union militiamen came looking for his

brother Frank. They grabbed Jesse and his stepfather and tied ropes around their necks. They beat Jesse with their sabers and nearly killed his stepfather by tightening the noose and "running him up" the tree to hang several times.

Before they left, the Union militia told Jesse that this was a warning. But that didn't sit well with him.

"After that day," said Frank, "Jesse was out for blood."

Frank, Jesse, and the Younger brothers soon honed their taste for violence under another notorious Quantrill leader— William "Bloody Bill" Anderson. Bloody Bill was known for wearing a necklace made of Yankee scalps and had a penchant for cutting off ears. In 1864, he led the James boys, Jim Younger, and the rest of his Raiders, into the small town of Centralia, Missouri, where they looted homes and savagely killed and mutilated more than one hundred unarmed Union soldiers who were on leave.

One month later, Union forces ambushed Bloody Bill. Union commander Samuel Cox killed him. And Jesse James vowed revenge, which he would exact on December 7, 1869, when he and his brother Frank robbed the Daviess County bank.

✕

Although the Civil War had officially ended four years earlier, for many Southern sympathizers like Jesse, their bitterness and antagonism raged on. So when Jesse, Frank, and Cole Younger robbed the Daviess County bank in

The last gun Jesse James used, a .45 Schofield, which could be loaded faster than any other guns of the day, using just one hand.

Gallatin, Missouri, and murdered the bank's president, it wasn't just about the money. It was also about vengeance. Jesse believed the bank's president was Samuel Cox, the killer of Bloody Bill.

But it turned out to be a case of mistaken identity. Jesse had killed the wrong man. Even though it wasn't the James-Younger Gang's first bank robbery or killing, it was the first time their names were printed in the newspaper, linking them to the crime.

Jesse swore up and down that he and his gang were innocent. The story grabbed the attention of John Edwards, an ex–Confederate soldier who was the editor of the *Kansas City Times*.

Despite the fact that the Confederacy had lost the war, Edwards's aim was to further their cause. He wanted ex-Confederates to feel proud and get back their political power. So Edwards made contact with the James boys and had Jesse write a public statement regarding the robbery. The statement was the start of Edwards's campaign to shape the public perception of Jesse James, transforming him from a villain into a noble Southern hero.

In the statement, Jesse declared his innocence and blamed the Unionists, who, in his opinion, were the real criminals in their relentless pursuit to punish the ex-Confederates. It read in part:

> *I well know if I was to submit to an arrest, that I would be mobbed and hanged without a trial. The past is sufficient to show that bushwhackers have been arrested in Missouri since the war, charged with bank robbery, and they most of all have been mobbed without trials. It is true that during the war I was a Confederate soldier, and fought under the black flag, but since then I have lived a peaceable citizen . . . As soon as I think I can get a just trial I will surrender myself to the civil authorities of Missouri and prove to the world that I am innocent of the crime charged against me.*

As time passed, suspicions waned, especially after Jesse and Frank's mom gave them an alibi.

Shy and studious, Frank James enjoyed reading Shakespeare.

So when Bob Pinkerton knocked on Zerelda's door to ask her questions about her boys, she cast a suspicious eye on the stranger. To Zerelda and many Southern sympathizers, her sons weren't outlaws; they were warriors and freedom fighters who were being persecuted by the Union.

Despite her wariness toward Bob, he pressed on, asking her questions. But Zerelda didn't give him any useful information—not even a description of what they looked like. She carefully guarded the only photos of her boys. Besides, she never knew where her sons were. While on the run from the law, they hid out in different towns, using fake names. And they always made sure not to tell her—just in case a stranger came knocking on her door asking about them.

Realizing it was futile, Bob left. He tried to continue the investigation, but with no good leads, the trail went cold. The Ocobock brothers finally gave up the hunt. Pinkerton was off the case. For now.

Chapter 13
Dead Man in the Road

Gads Hill, Missouri, January 31, 1874

It was close to five o'clock in the afternoon as the train thundered down the St. Louis and Iron Mountain railroad tracks, heading toward Poplar Bluff, Missouri. Looking out the window, the passengers could gaze at the dense woods, narrow valleys, deep gorges, and steep hills that were carpeted with brush and pine trees.

But clergyman Thomas Hagerty wasn't looking out the window. The scenery had quickly become monotonous. Instead, he was reading a good book. And it wasn't until the whistle blew and the train stopped at the Gads Hill station that he finally decided to put the book down and look out the window.

That's when he spotted a team of agitated horses hitched to a tree. Then he saw a man running. At first he thought the man was running to the horses to calm them down. But the man kept running, right past them, heading toward the train.

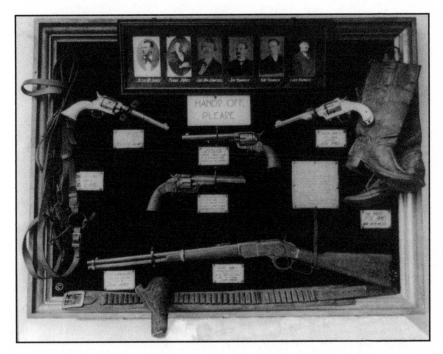

Jesse James's guns, boots, and equipment. Jesse always
made sure he was heavily armed.

And as he ran closer and closer, Hagerty saw that the man
was wearing a mask and holding a gun in his hand. Hagerty
opened the window, stuck his head out, looked to the left,
and saw the train's conductor standing on the platform. A
masked man was standing next to him, holding a pistol to
his head.

Hagerty rushed to the door and looked out. He saw several masked men in front of the train, and they were yelling.

"Go back into the car!"

"Keep your seats!"

"Shoot the first man that stirs!"

Hagerty quickly went back to his seat.

"I always want to live ready for a departure for the better world," said the clergyman. "But I did not see just then that these gentlemen were the proper ones to invite me to take that journey."

He listened to the two women sitting in front of him. One was traveling for the very first time to Missouri. The other was a widow with two children. Her six-year-old son asked, "Ma, where are the police?"

Some of the passengers were checking their pockets, while others were taking off their watches and hiding them under the seats. No one was armed.

Hagerty sat still in his seat and prayed until three men came into his car. Their revolvers were drawn.

"We are robbers," one of them said. "We want your money. Keep your seat or we will shoot."

Two of the robbers walked down between the rows of seats, making sure that the coast was clear. Afterward, they began to rob each passenger.

They stopped in front of each male passenger, held a gun to the man's head, and asked a series of questions.

"Who are you, sir? Where are you from? What is your business? Well, I will take your money."

If the amount was too small, the bandit said, "Is that all you got?" and threw it back. If it was a large amount, the bandit said, "You can spare me that." And he might check the rich man's pockets.

Hagerty, who was sitting in the middle of the passenger car, watched and worried. He wasn't sure how they would react to his being a minister, but he wasn't going to lie.

"Well, who are you?" the bandit asked.

"I am a minister, sir."

"Oh! Well, we don't want to disturb you!" said the masked bandit. "Boys, don't molest the minister; we will let him pass."

When the bandits approached the two women sitting in front of him, they bowed their heads politely.

"Don't be alarmed, ladies," said the bandit. "We will not disturb you."

After the last passenger was robbed, they left. But before one of the masked bandits stepped off, he spoke a few lines of Shakespeare with a dramatic flourish. And another one left behind a note. Using a pseudonym, Jesse James had written it especially for the newspapers.

> *The most daring robbery on record. The south bound train on the Iron Mountain railway was robbed here this evening by five heavily armed men and robbed of ———— dollars. The robbers arrived at the station a few minutes before the arrival of the train and arrested the agent, put him under guard and then threw the train on switch. The robbers were all large men, none of them under six feet tall, and all masked.*

They started in a southerly direction after they had
robbed the train, all on fine bred horses. There is a
hell of an excitement in this part of the country.
    (Signed)
    Ira A. Merrill

After all was said and done, the James-Younger Gang stole about $2,000 from the passengers and a large amount of jewelry. They also stole $1,000 from the Adams Express car. The Iron Mountain Railroad hired the Pinkerton Detective Agency to track down the bandits—last seen leaving in a southerly direction.

✕

When the hunt for the James-Younger Gang began, Allan Pinkerton had been back at his beloved detective agency for three years. He had returned to work in the fall of 1871. But things were different, himself included.

The once vibrant, danger-loving Pinkerton was still suffering from the damaging effects of the massive stroke. For the last two years, through sheer will, he had pushed himself to do punishing exercises to help him walk and talk. Little by little his speech improved. And he went from being in a wheelchair to walking with a cane—up to twelve miles a day.

"I am beating all the doctors," he wrote in a letter to a friend.

A family portrait of the Younger brothers with their sister. The Youngers were from a wealthy family. From left to right: Robert, Henrietta, Cole, and James.

But Pinkerton would never recover from one lasting effect of the stroke. It had forced him to slow down and relinquish some control of his detective agency. His sons, Bob and Billy, now had larger roles. Billy was in charge of the Chicago office, which covered the midwestern and western states. Bob was in charge of the New York office, which opened in 1866. He oversaw operations in the southern and eastern states.

Nevertheless, there was no mistaking who was really in charge—Allan Pinkerton. Clearly, the stroke had affected his physical strength, but his spirit and personality were still just as fierce as ever. Pinkerton summed it up in a letter he wrote to a new employee:

> *I rule my office with an iron hand. I am self-willed and obstinate . . . I must have my **own way of doing things**.*

No sooner had Pinkerton returned to work when tragedy struck again. On October 8, 1871, the Great Chicago Fire blazed ruthlessly through the city, burning most of it to the ground. Pinkerton's National Detective Agency was no exception. The fire destroyed all of Pinkerton's Civil War records and criminal case files, including his prized Rogues' Gallery that contained photos and descriptions of wanted criminals.

It was a devastating setback. But Pinkerton was ready to

fight. While the building was still smoldering, he hired a team of carpenters to rebuild it.

"I will never be beaten, never. Not all the Furies of Hell will stop me from rebuilding <u>immediately</u>," Pinkerton wrote to his loyal friend and employee George Bangs.

Within a year, Pinkerton's National Detective Agency was rebuilt.

While Pinkerton was rebuilding his life, Jesse James was busy building his public image. In the three years since Pinkerton's last investigation, Jesse's reputation as a hero had grown into a mythic, Robin Hood–like image. His targets were greedy and ruthless bankers and railroad tycoons. He continued to contact newspapers, declaring his innocence and stating, "We are not thieves—we are bold robbers . . . [we] rob the rich and give to the poor."

But not everyone believed it, especially those, like the Pinkertons, who came into contact with the gang.

"I consider Jesse James the worst man, without exception, in America," wrote Bob Pinkerton. "He is utterly devoid of fear, and has no more compunction about cold blooded murder than he has about eating his breakfast."

Billy Pinkerton agreed, calling him a "blood-thirsty devil."

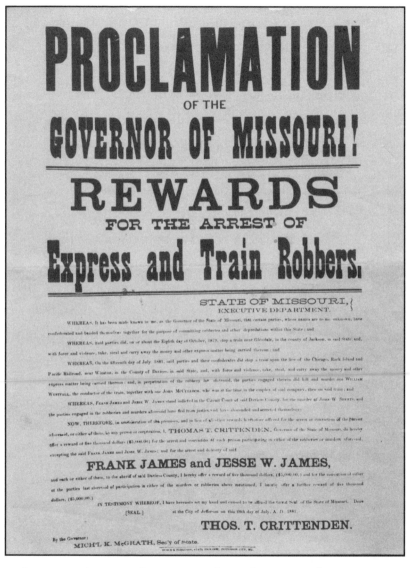

The wanted poster for Jesse and Frank James. There weren't any photos of the outlaws, so Pinkerton detectives didn't know what they looked like.

On March 10, 1874, about a month after the Gads Hill robbery, the morning train pulled into Liberty, Missouri, and a tall, well-built man with blue eyes and a light mustache stepped off. He was a stranger in this part of the country, hailing from Iowa City where he lived with his wife. He had traveled the world when he was a sailor on a ship, transporting fruit back and forth from New York to the Mediterranean region.

But he was forced to change jobs when he fell from the ship's masthead and broke his ankle. After that, twenty-six-year-old Joseph Whicher went to work for Allan Pinkerton.

For the past three years, Joseph Whicher had worked for Pinkerton's National Detective Agency, where he had proven himself to be a shrewd and discreet undercover detective. Pinkerton had chosen him to infiltrate the James-Younger Gang.

Whicher's first order of business after arriving in Liberty was to stop at the bank. He wanted to make a deposit. He knew full well that it was a bad idea to carry a lot of cash, especially in James-Younger territory.

After making the deposit, Whicher met with George Patton, Clay County's sheriff. Whicher confided in him that he was heading toward Zerelda Samuel's farm. He had heard they needed some help, and he wanted to work as a farmhand as a way of infiltrating the James-Younger Gang.

Since there weren't any photos of the James boys, Whicher asked for a description and directions to the farm. The sheriff warned him that it was a bad idea. If he was discovered and the James boys didn't kill him, then their mother would—she was a "dead shot." But Whicher wasn't afraid of the James boys. And he set off for the farm.

The next morning, on March 11, about ten miles away in Independence, Missouri, a laborer was driving his horse-drawn wagon, carrying a load of wood, when he suddenly stopped. He was at a fork in the road, the point where Lexington, Liberty, and Independence Roads crossed. There was a dead man lying in the road. His hands and feet were tied. The dead man's body was shot all to pieces. The dead man was Joseph Whicher.

The coroner was notified, and he examined the body. Whicher's hat had been tied to his head with a handkerchief. He had a bullet hole in his temple. The pistol had been fired so close to his head that the handkerchief had burn marks. He was also shot through the neck, in his shoulder, and in his leg.

At the inquest, a jury gave the verdict "death from gunshot wounds at the hands of persons unknown." But everyone knew who did it, only no one was talking. The James boys had made sure of that.

Chapter 14
The Final Showdown

Clay County, Missouri, March 12, 1874

The day after Whicher's dead body was found, the James boys rode their horses into town and threatened people.

"Talking about this murder and connecting our names to it. We will blow your d—d head off," they said.

Their threats worked. The citizens in Clay County were silenced. The *Rocky Mountain News* reported:

> *These men have established a perfect terrorism in their neighborhood. Everybody is afraid of them. People will not talk about the murder—or, if they do, it is only in low tones and in the seclusion of back rooms.*

When the Pinkertons heard the news about Whicher, they were certain that Sheriff Patton had betrayed them by tipping off the James boys. It turned out that the sheriff had been a schoolmate of theirs.

"We established the fact beyond all cavil that two hours after Whicher made known his stratagem to the sheriff, that the official was seen to stealthily enter the house of the [Samuel] family and forewarn them of the trap that was being laid for the [James] boys," said Bob Pinkerton.

The sheriff emphatically denied it, calling Bob a "villainous slanderer and falsifier."

About a week after Whicher's murder, Pinkerton sent Louis Lull, a former captain of the Chicago police, to go after the James-Younger Gang. Lull brought a former St. Louis police officer named John Boyle with him. Together, they traveled to St. Clair County, Missouri, in the Ozarks, where the Younger brothers' well-respected relatives lived. Once there, Lull hired Edwin Daniels, a former deputy sheriff, to accompany them.

On March 16, at 2:30 p.m., Lull was on a white horse, riding next to Daniels, and Boyle was riding a short distance in front of them. They had just stopped by the home of Theodore Snuffer, a distant relative of the Youngers. Pretending to be cattle buyers, they asked for directions to the Simms place, saying they heard the widow had some cattle to sell. Snuffer gave them directions.

However, Pinkerton's men didn't know that John and Jim Younger happened to be at Snuffer's house, hiding, and heard the whole conversation. The Younger brothers watched the strangers leave, and when they saw that the strangers weren't following Snuffer's directions, it raised their suspicions.

Pinkerton's men were on the road heading toward Chalk Level, Missouri, about a mile from Snuffer's farm, when they heard some noise behind them. They looked back and saw two men on horseback coming toward them. They didn't know the men were John and Jim Younger, but one had his double-barreled shotgun cocked, and the other was carrying a revolver. They told Lull and the others to halt and surrender.

Lull turned his horse around and threw his pistol down.

"All right, boys, what is it?" said Lull.

Boyle, who was still ahead of them, pulled out his pistol, put spurs to his horse, and took off. The Younger brothers told him to halt, but he didn't. So Jim Younger went after him, firing his gun. Boyle's hat was shot off his head, but he wasn't hurt. So he kept on going, riding as fast as he could.

Without warning, Lull drew his gun, cocked it, and fired. The bullet hit John Younger in the neck, ripping open his jugular vein. At nearly the same moment, John fired both barrels of his shotgun at Lull. The shots tore into his left arm and chest. Lull's frightened horse took off into the bushes and ran toward the nearby trees.

John Younger quickly turned toward Daniels and fired a revolver, killing him on the spot.

Holding the reins with his right hand, Lull desperately tried to regain control of his horse. But John Younger fired two more shots at him, one of them tearing through Lull's stomach. Lull's horse kept going into the brush, and Lull fell out of the saddle. He got up, staggered across the road, and fell to the ground. Dead.

✕

Two days later, on March 18, the newspaper reported that a dead man was found lying in the road with a bloody note pinned to his coat. It was written by Jesse and Frank James, warning Pinkerton that this was "the fate of all Pinkerton's detectives."

Although the dead man's identity was never confirmed, the message was loud and clear. There would be more bloodshed.

✕

The James-Younger Gang had killed two of Pinkerton's detectives within a week. Pinkerton was seething and out for blood. A month later, on April 17, 1874, Pinkerton wrote to George Bangs:

> *I know that the James-Youngers are desperate men, and that if we meet it must be the death of one or both of us . . . my blood was spilt and they must repay . . . there is no use talking, they must die.*

✕

On January 26, 1875, eight Pinkerton detectives, all armed with weapons, trudged through the wet snow with several

The Jameses' family farm, where the raid occurred.

trustworthy Clay County citizens. It was a cold night, but the moon was bright in the clear sky.

The men crept quietly in the dark, making their way to Zerelda Samuel's farm. Earlier that evening, Allan and Billy Pinkerton, who were supervising the operation from Chicago, had been assured in a telegram that the James boys were in town visiting their mother and staying at her house.

"I had given positive orders that no harm was to be done to the women or Dr. Samuel, and no one else [who] was there," Pinkerton wrote in a letter.

It was midnight when Pinkerton's men finally reached the farm. Hiding behind the icehouse, without saying a word,

Zerelda Samuel, mother of American outlaws
Jesse and Frank James.

they prepared for their raid. A half hour later, two men lit a fireball and rushed toward the house. They smashed in a boarded-up window and threw the flaming fireball into the kitchen.

Inside, smoke filled the room. Screams rang out. Zerelda and her husband, Reuben, jumped out of bed and ran into the kitchen. Their children followed.

When Zerelda saw "a bowl of fire in the middle of the floor," she tried to pick it up, but it was too heavy. Desperate, she tried to kick it into the fireplace with her foot, but it wouldn't move. Her husband grabbed a shovel, scooped it up, and threw it into the fireplace onto the burning embers. This was a grave mistake.

The fireball exploded. Metal shrapnel flew through the air. One piece sliced Zerelda's arm, her hand hanging by a thread, and another killed her eight-year-old son, Archie.

✕

The plan to capture the James boys didn't go at all as planned. And the Pinkerton men were shocked even further when they learned that the James boys weren't in the house—they'd left the day before—some said they were tipped off.

The biggest controversy was the explosion. Jesse's family called it a bomb, and the Clay County newspaper called "the act . . . not only indefensible but cowardly and barbarous."

The Pinkertons vehemently denied it was a bomb.

"It was no more a bomb than a kerosene lamp would be . . . The so-called bomb was one of several made at Rock Island Arsenal. It was a metallic case or shell stuffed with lampwick and soaked in coal oil," said Billy Pinkerton.

Despite the robberies and murders the James-Younger Gang had committed, the fireball explosion garnered an outpouring of sympathy for the James family and a tirade against the Pinkertons. The *Kansas City Times* newspaper printed a scathing editorial with the blaring headline, PINKERTON'S VENDETTA. It read in part:

PINKERTON determined to avenge the death of his men. He sent a force to surround the residence of DR. SAMUEL at night, hoping to find the JAMES boys there, but determined anyhow to leave his mark and take a terrible vengeance on the family . . . But no JAMES boys appeared, and PINKERTON's braves, not daring to meet the responsibility of their savage act, fled away to the special train which was to carry them beyond the reach of outraged law. But in this case justice looks only to the fact that the cowardly vengeance of baffled detectives makes indiscriminate war on a whole family.

Although there was sympathy, many in Clay County were terrified, especially after one of Zerelda's neighbors was found murdered. He was killed for helping Pinkerton's men. Clay County sheriff John Groom wrote to Missouri governor Charles Henry Hardin.

"The citizens . . . are greatly terror stricken as anytime during the war . . . There are many men here now who expect to meet and share the same fate. There is no doubt about the threats against them by the James brothers and their associates."

Jesse openly vowed vengeance against the Pinkertons. In a letter to the *Nashville Banner* newspaper, Jesse wrote:

[Pinkerton] may vindicate himself with some, but he better never dare show his Scottish face again

in Western Mo . . . or he will meet the fate of his comrades, Capt. Lull & Whicher . . . Joe Witchers [sic] came to Clay County, Mo . . . and went to the honorable sheriff . . . with ten thousand lies, and that night he was kidnapped and got his just deserts; and it was in revenge for that the Pinkerton force tried to destroy an innocent, helpless family.

It was reported that Jesse even went to Chicago with hopes to kill Allan.

"I could have killed the younger one but I didn't," said Jesse. "I wanted him to know who did it. It wouldn't do me no good if I couldn't tell him about it before he died."

✕

In March, a grand jury in Clay County was investigating the raid.

"I have but little to say about this subject," Pinkerton wrote to his son Bob. "The fact is they are trying their best to get indictments against some of my men for the operation in Clay County where James's mother had met with a merited and fearful punishment."

The grand jury indicted eight Pinkerton detectives, including Allan, for the murder of Archie Samuel. But no one was ever arrested. There wasn't enough hard evidence, and the charges were dismissed.

The James-Younger Gang continued to rob and kill. In

1876, the gang robbed the First National Bank in Northfield, Minnesota. Before leaving, Frank or Jesse shot and killed an unarmed bookkeeper. Only Frank and Jesse would escape that day. The citizens of Northfield banded together, shot back, and hunted the rest of the gang down, capturing the Younger brothers. Unlike Frank, William, and Simeon Reno, the Younger brothers did not get lynched, for which they were grateful.

That same year, Jesse's image as a hero began to fade. Newspaper editor John Edwards had no need to publish his letters and perpetuate an image of a Southern hero. After Rutherford Hayes was elected president, the federal troops in the South were removed, and ex-Confederates had their political power back. The period of Reconstruction was over.

By 1882, after more robberies and killings of unarmed citizens, Jesse's image as an outlaw was sealed when a large reward was offered for his capture. On April 3, a member of Jesse's own gang, Bob Ford, shot him in the back of the head while he was dusting a picture on the wall. Ford was granted immunity and received the reward money as part of a pre-arranged deal with the governor.

Fearing the same fate, Jesse's brother Frank surrendered shortly after. He went on trial three times. Each jury came back with the same verdict. Not guilty.

X

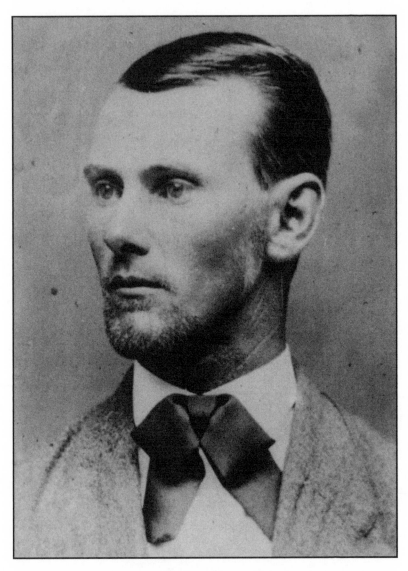

A rare photo of Jesse James.

For Allan Pinkerton, Jesse James would always be the outlaw who not only tarnished his good reputation but the one who also got away. After the bloodshed and fury, Pinkerton decided to give up the hunt for the outlaws.

In a letter to his son Bob, Pinkerton wrote, "I paid the penalty of having lost my men but I will not bandy words regarding those great men in the detective business. . . . I must say my end is accomplished and in that I am content."

Chapter 15
End of Days

1874–1884

During the time that Pinkerton was chasing down Jesse James and his gang, he was also in charge of another explosive case. In 1874, the Philadelphia & Reading Railroad hired Pinkerton's National Detective Agency to bring down the Molly Maguires, a secret Irish-American organization that was blamed for the high rate of murders in the coal-mining towns of Pennsylvania.

At the time, many considered the Molly Maguires to be terrorists, beating and killing anyone who opposed them. But others considered them to be like a labor union that rebelled against the horrendous working conditions that coal miners endured.

Pinkerton sent his undercover detective James McParland to the dangerous coal-mining towns in Pennsylvania. In May 1877, more than seventy suspected members of the Molly Maguires were rounded up and arrested. Twenty-three were sentenced to die—and ten were hanged on June 21.

At the time of the hangings, Pinkerton and McParland were praised and highly regarded for their work in ending the Molly Maguires and their "reign of blood." *The American Law Review* stated:

> *The debt which the coal counties owe to these men cannot be overestimated, nor can the personal qualities of untiring resolution, daring and sagacity, in both principal and agents be too highly praised.*

But the years of chasing criminals and the effects of the stroke had taken a toll on Pinkerton. Still walking with a cane, Pinkerton was now slightly stooped and his hands shook from palsy. Against his will, he could no longer go out in the field and hunt down criminals.

And that irritated him to no end.

Nevertheless, Pinkerton continued to go into his Chicago office to check reports, give orders, and direct the business. He was still a great crime solver—just from behind his desk.

In 1879, he received a letter from his son Bob, outlining a case he was working on. Grave robbers had stolen the dead body of Alexander Stewart, a famous business tycoon. Typical of the day, the thieves demanded money in exchange for the return of the body. They had refused the $25,000 offered. Bob needed Pinkerton's advice on the matter.

The fact is Robert, from all this seeming correspon-
dence, I think the body is not far away. You will notice
they talk about the annoyances of the Custom House
officers in having the body brought from Canada,
but they forgot to mention any annoyance to them
whilst taking the remains to Canada. No, I do not
think this story of the body being taken to Canada
hangs well together; I think the remains may be in
New Jersey or at farthest, in Pennsylvania.

Pinkerton was right. The body was not in Canada. It was eventually recovered in New York in exchange for a $20,000 ransom.

✕

Although Pinkerton still enjoyed spending time in his Chicago office, on Fridays, he often went on weekend retreats to his 254-acre estate, the Larches, about eighty miles outside of Chicago. He rode the Illinois Central train, which had a special stop right outside his estate.

Throughout Pinkerton's career, there were always threats against his life. But after the Molly Maguires case, the threats of murder and bombings had intensified. So Pinkerton kept armed guards on duty around the clock. A long driveway, lined with Larch trees imported from Scotland, circled around the white-pillared main house

The main house at the Larches. The cupola on top of the house is where an armed guard scanned the area for would-be assassins.

where guards manned the lookout tower. As an added precaution, Pinkerton always slept with his six-shooter.

Pinkerton often invited friends to the Larches. Visitors included former Union general and president Ulysses S. Grant, railroad tycoon Cornelius Vanderbilt, and Adams Express president Henry Sanford. While there, they could enjoy riding horses, swimming in the pool, fishing in the pond, or relaxing with a bottle of wine from Pinkerton's wine cellar that he called the Snuggery.

When Pinkerton wasn't entertaining guests, he was busy working on his books. He dictated his stories, based on his years as a detective, to an assistant who typed up an outline and sent them to the publisher. Ghost writers filled in the details, and parts of his books were fictionalized, but they were always bestsellers.

Although Pinkerton had cut back on the number of hours he spent in his Chicago office, and his sons were helping him run the business, he was still very much in charge of Pinkerton's National Detective Agency. Any decisions regarding running the company had to pass by Pinkerton. This was especially evident when George Bangs and Pinkerton's son Bob wanted the agency to stop hiring woman detectives. Pinkerton fired off an angry letter.

It has been my principle to use females for the detection of crime where it has been useful and necessary . . . with regard to the employment of such females, I can trace it back to the time I first hired Kate Warne, up to the present time . . . and I intend to still use females whenever it can be done judiciously. I must do it or falsify my theory, practice and truth.

When Bob wrote back, pushing the issue again, Pinkerton gave his final reply.

I return your letter as it is disrespectful to me as the Principal of this Agency. It is doubly . . . triply disrespectful to me as your father . . . For the last time I shall tell you that you have no right to interfere with the employment of any Agency, except those of New York, of which you are Superintendent . . . After I am dead and the sod is growing over my grave you will then learn that someone must take the management of everything, but while I live I mean to be the Principal of this Agency.

The matter was settled. Pinkerton ruled at work. But the detective agency wasn't his only concern.

✕

At home, he was worried about his wife's failing health. Joan had become terribly ill and was bedridden. He loved her dearly and cut back on his hours at the office so he could be with her. Pinkerton wanted to stay by her side "listening to her every word."

While she was recovering, Pinkerton wrote a loving letter to her on their thirty-fifth wedding anniversary:

> *You have been battling with me, side by side, willing to do anything, to bear our children and work hard, yet you never found fault, you never said a cross word but was always willing to make our home cheery and happy . . . Now Joan, on this day, I wish you to take things easy. When I can get home I will come and sit by you and talk to you and cheer you . . . Let us wish we may be spared a few more years . . . enjoying happiness and health to ourselves, our children and our friends.*

Pinkerton and his wife had several more years together, until the summer of 1884. Early one morning, while Pinkerton was out taking his daily walk, he stumbled and lost his balance. Hitting the ground hard, Pinkerton bit his tongue and developed gangrene, making him dangerously ill.

His son Billy and his daughter, Joan, never left his bedside. Pinkerton didn't regain consciousness. Three weeks later, on July 1, sixty-four-year-old Allan Pinkerton, America's first private eye, was dead.

The news of his death made headlines. The newspaper hailed him as "the great detective" and "a bitter foe to the rogues." Pinkerton had blazed the trail for detective and spy work.

And to this day, his legacy continues.

Epilogue
Pinkerton's Legacy

Pinkerton's National Detective Agency was passed down to his sons, Billy and Bob. Together, they grew the family business. Under their leadership, the agency continued to hunt down nearly every major bank and train robber—including Butch Cassidy and the Sundance Kid.

Billy became a celebrated detective, just like his father. In 1901, he brought international recognition to the agency when he recovered the famous painting of the Duchess of Devonshire, which had been stolen from a London art gallery twenty-six years earlier.

Pinkerton's National Detective Agency was highly regarded by London's Metro Police, also known as Scotland Yard, especially after helping capture the notorious Bidwell brothers, who had stolen more than one million dollars from the Bank of England. In 1911, Scotland Yard invited Billy to study the new art of fingerprinting as a method of identifying criminals at a crime scene. When Billy returned to the United States, he was the leader in promoting its efficiency and superiority over any other method.

Fingerprinting wasn't the only big change for Pinkerton's National Detective Agency. The creation of the Federal Bureau of Investigation (FBI) in 1908 had an impact on their business. Local police could now turn to the FBI to investigate interstate crimes—no longer needing Pinkerton detectives to work in the role of a nationwide police force.

Even so, Allan Pinkerton's "fingerprints" were all over the creation of the FBI. It didn't take a detective to see that Pinkerton was a major influence on the FBI's operations as well as law enforcement in general. To this day, they continue to use Allan Pinkerton's pioneering methods of investigation—shadowing suspects and using disguises to go undercover. They also keep detailed records of criminals, just like Allan Pinkerton's original and highly prized Rogues' Gallery, which was his collection of criminal mug shots, biographies, and methods of operations. In fact, Pinkerton's Rogues' Gallery was the basis for the FBI's Criminal Identification Bureau.

Despite the loss of business, Pinkerton's National Detective Agency had already begun adapting to the changing times. Although the agency continued to do detective work, in the 1890s, they began shifting the main focus of their business away from crime solving to crime prevention. To do this, they began growing their guard and security division. It wasn't long before the name "Pinkerton" also became synonymous with "armed guard."

Big companies regularly hired Pinkerton guards to break

up strikes, which oftentimes resulted in violence. As a result, labor unions and laborers despised them. In 1892, Pinkerton guards were called in during the Homestead Strike in Pennsylvania. When they arrived, a battle erupted, leaving three strikers and seven Pinkerton guards dead and many more wounded.

The incident ignited controversy, tarnishing the agency's reputation and nearly ruining the company. Soon after, the agency no longer accepted any cases involving labor unions and strikebreaking.

Despite the controversy, Pinkerton's National Detective Agency recovered and, throughout the years, continued to thrive. Bob proved to be a shrewd business administrator. He negotiated one of the largest contracts ever for the agency when three thousand banks formed an alliance and hired them to provide security, with an eye on preventing robberies, forgeries, and swindles.

Their business also provided protection and investigative services against jewel thieves for the major jewelry companies. And racetracks were also a big moneymaking customer. The racetracks hired Pinkerton guards against pickpockets, ticket forgers, and drunks. Cheating was also a problem. So Pinkerton's National Detective Agency created a horse-identification system to thwart "ringers," so a slow horse couldn't be substituted with a fast look-alike horse.

"The work we are engaged in now is, of course, of quite another sort," Billy said in an interview. "It takes more brains and less muscle, although we have some good hard fights to fight, too."

When Billy was asked what his father would think of the changing business, he replied, "Why! Nothing ever really surprised Father."

✕

Pinkerton's National Detective Agency remained a family business until 1967, when Allan Pinkerton's great-grandson stepped down as the head of the agency. That same year, the company, which was renamed Pinkerton's, Inc. to reflect its focus on security, went public, allowing outside investors to buy shares of the company.

In 1982, Pinkerton's was sold to American Brands, a huge corporation. Six years later, the company changed hands again when its archrival, California Plant Protection (CPP), acquired Pinkerton's. In 1999, Securitas, a Swedish company, bought Pinkerton's, making it the largest security firm in the world. Renamed Pinkerton Consulting & Investigations, they still perform undercover operations.

And to think, it all began when a cooper needed some wood to make his barrels.

Source Notes

Alexander, Ted. "Battle of Antietam." *Civil War Times,* September 2006.

Andreas, A. T. *History of Chicago: From the Earliest to the Present Time.* Chicago: A. T. Andreas, Publisher, 1884.

Arnold, Isaac Newton. "The Baltimore Plot to Assassinate Abraham Lincoln." *Harper's New Monthly Magazine,* June 1868.

Aspen Tribune. No Title. November 10, 1895. (Article is about Robert Pinkerton.)

Barbour County Index (Medicine Lodge, KS). "A Life of Crime." August 4, 1881.

Bell, William. "Reno Gang's Reign of Terror." *Wild West,* February 2004.

Benjamin, Philip. " 'They Never Sleep'; Pinkerton's 'Private Eyes' Have Been on Duty for More Than a Hundred Years." *New York Times Magazine,* August 27, 1961.

Beymer, William Gilmore. "Timothy Webster: Spy." *Harper's Monthly Magazine,* Vol. CXXI, June to November, New York: Harper & Brothers, 1910.

Bowman, Tom. "Antietam: A Savage Day in American History." NPR.org, September 17, 2012.

Brown, George William. *Baltimore and the Nineteenth of April, 1861: A Study of War.* Baltimore: John Hopkins University, 1887.

Cambridge Jeffersonian (OH). "Western Banditti." November 9, 1876.

Centerville Citizen (IA). "Bold Robbery at Corydon." June 10, 1871.

Chicago Tribune. "Allan Pinkerton." July 2, 1884.

———. "The Bank and Railroad Robbers." July 31, 1873.

———. "Deputy Officer Shot!" September 9, 1853.

———. "Eye That Never Sleeps." June 30, 1890.

———. "The Younger Boys." March 27, 1875.

Cincinnati Enquirer. "Detroit." October 16, 1868.

———. "Famous Western Bandits." July 6, 1907.

———. "Lynch Law." December 14, 1868.

———. "Missouri's Bold Bandits." November 22, 1879.

———. "The New Albany Tragedy." December 15, 1868.

Colbert, Elias and Everett Chamberlin. *Chicago and the Great Conflagration.* Cincinnati and New York: C.F. Vent, 1871.

Colbert, Thomas Burnell. "Dean, Henry Clay." *The Biographical Dictionary of Iowa.* University of Iowa Press, 2009. Web. March 3, 2014.

Colorado Banner (Boulder, CO). "Pinkerton's Men." October 21, 1875.

The Courier-Journal (Louisville, KY). "Allan Pinkerton." August 12, 1884.

———. "Laura Reno." December 25, 1868.

———. "The Train Robbers." February 6, 1874.

Crawford, Amy. "Outlaw Hunters." Smithsonian.com, August 31, 2007.

Crook, Mary Charlotte. "Rose O'Neale Greenhow, Confederate Spy." *The Montgomery County Story*, Vol. 32, No. 2, May 1989.

Currey, J. Seymour. *Chicago: Its History and Its Builders.* Chicago: S.J. Clarke, 1912.

Cuthbert, Norma B. *Lincoln and the Baltimore Plot, 1861: From Pinkerton Records and Related Papers.* San Marino, CA: Huntington Library, 1949.

Daily Democratic Press (Chicago). "Officer Shot." September 9, 1853.

Dempsey, John S. and Linda S. Forst. *An Introduction to Policing.* 5th ed. Clifton Park, NY: Delmar, Cengage Learning, 2010.

Drayton, H. S. and N. Sizer. "Allan Pinkerton, the Detective." *The Phrenological Journal* 79, no. 8 (September 1884): 121–24.

Elyria Republican (OH). "Allan Pinkerton." July 10, 1884.

Evening Telegraph (Philadelphia). "A Whole Family of Robbers in Indiana." July 17, 1868.

Fishel, Edwin C. *The Secret War for the Union: The Untold Story of Military Intelligence in the Civil War.* Boston: Houghton Mifflin, 1996.

Flinn, John J. *History of the Chicago Police.* Chicago: Under the Auspices of the Police Book Fund, 1887.

Fort Wayne Daily Gazette. "The Clandestine Journey." May 31, 1866.

———. "The New Albany Tragedy." December 15, 1868.

Gale, Edwin Oscar. *Reminiscences of Early Chicago and Vicinity*. Chicago: Fleming H. Revell, 1902.

Greenhow, Mrs. (Rose). *My Imprisonment and the First Year of Abolition Rule at Washington*. London: Richard Bentley, 1863.

Harrisburg Telegraph. "Pinkerton on Guard." December 11, 1886.

Horan, James D. *The Pinkertons: The Detective Dynasty That Made History*. New York: Bonanza, 1967.

Inglis, William. "A Republic's Gratitude: What Pryce Lewis Did for the United States Government, and How the United States Government Rewarded Him." *Harper's Weekly* 55, no. 2871 (December 30, 1911): 24.

Indianapolis News. "A History of the Renos." July 8, 1895.

Inter Ocean (Chicago). "Recalls Great Theft." July 9, 1899.

———. "Reminiscences." September 1, 1882.

James, Jr., Jesse. *Jesse James, My Father: The First and Only True Story of His Adventures Ever Written*. Cleveland: Buckeye, 1899.

Josephson, Judith Pinkerton. *Allan Pinkerton: The Original Private Eye*. Minneapolis: Lerner, 1996.

Joslyn, R. Waite and Frank W. Joslyn. *History of Kane County, Ill*. Vol. I. Chicago: Pioneer, 1908.

Kansas City Star. "R. A. Pinkerton Dies at Sea." August 17, 1907.

Klein, Christopher. "7 Ways the Battle of Antietam Changed America." History.com, September 14, 2012.

Lavine, Sigmund A. *Allan Pinkerton: America's First Private Eye*. London: Mayflower, 1963.

Lewin, Tamar. "Pinkerton's Is Being Acquired." *New York Times*, December 8, 1982.

Liberty Tribune. "Another Lie." April 24, 1874.

——. "The Men of Gad's Hill—A Fight with Them in Arkansas." April 17, 1874.

MacKay, James. *Allan Pinkerton: The First Private Eye.* New York: John Wiley & Sons, 1997.

Moffett, Cleveland. "Allan Pinkerton." *The Atlanta Constitution.* March 24, 1895.

——. "The Destruction of the Reno Gang." *McClure's Magazine* IV, December 1894–May 1895.

——. "How Allan Pinkerton Thwarted the First Plot to Assassinate Lincoln." *McClure's Magazine* III, June 1894–November 1894.

Morn, Frank. *The Eye That Never Sleeps: A History of the Pinkerton National Detective Agency.* Bloomington, IN: Indiana University, 1982.

Mortimer, Gavin. *Double Death: The True Story of Pryce Lewis, the Civil War's Most Daring Spy.* New York: Bloomsbury, 2010.

The National Cyclopædia of American Biography: Being the History of the United States. Vol. III. New York: James T. White, 1893.

National Park Service. "The Battle of Antietam." 2014. PDF file.

New York Times. "Allan Pinkerton: An Alleged Conspiracy Agained the Detective's Life." August 5, 1869.

——. "Allan Pinkerton's Death: The Career of the Great Detective Ended." July 1, 1884.

——. "Article 4—No Title." December 12, 1923. (Article is about William Pinkerton's death.)

——. "Death of Gen. M'Clellan." October 30, 1885.

——. "The Inauguration Ceremonies: The New Administration: March 5, 1861.

——. "The Pinkerton Conspiracy." August 24, 1869.

——. "Pinkerton's London Trip." July 23, 1911.

——. "A Remarkable Detective: Work of the Late George Henry Bangs." September 15, 1883.

——. "Robert A. Pinkerton, Chairman of Detective Agency, Is Dead." October 12, 1967.

——. "The Seymour Thieves." July 25, 1868.

——. "The Seymour Thieves." July 31, 1868.

——. "William Pinkerton Dies in California." December 12, 1923.

New-York Tribune. "Attempt at Wholesale Murder." August 2, 1855.

Palmer, Stanley H. "Cops and Guns: Arming the American Police." *History Today* 28, no. 6 (1976): 382–9.

Pierce, Bessie Louise. *A History of Chicago, Volume I: The Beginning of a City 1673–1848.* Chicago: University of Chicago, 2007.

Pinkerton, Allan. *Criminal Reminiscences and Detective Sketches.* New York: G. W. Dillingham, 1878.

——. *The Expressman and the Detective.* Chicago: W. B. Keen, Cooke, 1874.

——. *History and Evidence of the Passage of Abraham Lincoln from*

Harrisburg, Pa., to Washington, D.C., on the 22d and 23d of February, 1861. Chicago: Republican Print, 1868.

———. *The Rail-Road Forger and the Detectives.* New York: G. W. Carleton, 1881.

———. *The Spy of the Rebellion.* New York: G. W. Dillingham, 1883.

Pinkerton, Allan and George H. Bangs. *General Principles of Pinkerton's National Police Agency.* Chicago: Geo. H. Fergus, 1867.

Pinkerton, William A. "Highwaymen of the Railroad." *North American Review* 157 (November 1893).

"The 'Reno Gang.'" *History of Jackson County, Indiana.* Chicago: Brant & Fuller, 1886.

Richmond Daily Dispatch. "The Condemned Spies." April 5, 1862.

———. "Exodus from the County Jail." March 20, 1862.

———. "Recaptured." March 24, 1862.

———. "Trial Sentence, and Execution of Timothy Webster as a Spy." April 30, 1862.

Rix, Alice. "King of the Sleuths: A Study of the Modern Detective." *San Francisco Call* 84, no. 145 (October 23, 1898).

Rocky Mountain News. "Missouri. Another Detective Assassinated." April 21, 1874.

———. No Title. March 24, 1874. (Article is about Joseph Whicher and Jesse James.)

Rowan, Richard Wilmer. *The Pinkertons: A Detective Dynasty.* New York: Little, Brown, 1931.

Sacramento Daily Union. "Desperate Attempts to Assassinate Allan Pinkerton." October 29, 1869.

Schouler, William. *A History of Massachusetts in the Civil War.* Boston: E. P. Dutton, 1868.

Semi-Weekly Wisconsin (Milwaukee). "Mrs. Kate Warne, the Female Detective." March 11, 1868.

——. "The Tragedy in Indiana." December 19, 1868.

Smalley, George W. "Battle-Field of Antietam." *New-York Tribune,* September 17, 1862.

Soltysiak, H. A. "The Pinkerton Bomb." *American History Illustrated* 27, issue 2 (May/June 1992): 52.

South Haven Sentinel (MI). "The Gad's Hill Robbers." March 28, 1874.

Streeter, Kurt. "Troubled Pinkerton's Finds Safe Haven in Swedish Firm Securitas." *Los Angeles Times,* February 23, 1999.

Sycamore True Republican. "Allan Pinkerton." July 9, 1884.

——. "Wm. Pinkerton, Detective, Was Born in Dundee." December 15, 1923.

Times-Picayune (New Orleans). "An American Vidocq." June 29, 1860.

——. "An Attempt to Kill Detective Pinkerton." October 20, 1868.

Titusville Herald (PA). "The Renos." February 1, 1869.

The War of the Rebellion: A Compilation of the Official Records of the Union and Confederate Armies. Series I, Vol. XIX, Part I (Reports), Washington: Government Printing Office, 1897, 53, 65.

The War of the Rebellion: A Compilation of the Official Records of the Union and Confederate Armies. Series I, Vol. LI, Part II (Confederate Correspondence, Etc.), Washington: Government Printing Office, 1897, 688.

The War of the Rebellion: A Compilation of the Official Records of the Union and Confederate Armies. Series II, Vol. II, Part I (Prisoners of War), Washington: Government Printing Office, 1897, 35, 566–9.

Washington Times. "Great Detective Dies: 'Bob' Pinkerton's Life Ends During Sea Trip." August 18, 1907.

Weekly Era (Raleigh, NC). "Mail Train on Iron Mountain Railroad in Missouri." February 5, 1874.

The West Film Project and WETA. "William Clarke Quantrill." PBS.org. PBS, Web. March 3, 2014.

WGBH Educational Foundation. *American Experience: Jesse James*. PBS.org. PBS, Web. March 3, 2014.

Whittemore, Henry. *The Heroes of the American Revolution and Their Descendants*. New York: Heroes of the Revolution, 1897.

Wybrow, Robert J. *"My Arm Was Hanging Loose": The Pinkerton Attack on the James' Family Home*. London: English Westerners' Society, 2005.

INDEX

Page numbers in boldface indicate illustrations or photographs.

ACKNOWLEDGMENTS

It's no mystery that a big thank-you is due to many people—

To the Literary Gang: Marisa Polansky, Tod Olson, Kelly Smith, and Jessica Regel.

To the Library Gang: Lewis Wyman and Bruce Kirby at the Library of Congress, Jan Perone at the Abraham Lincoln Presidential Library, Paul Haggett at St. Lawrence University, and Amanda Schriver at the Newberry Library.

And a heartfelt thank-you to my husband, Todd, who has stories of his father, who was an undercover detective, leaving the house in disguise to hunt down the bad guys.

About the Author

SAMANTHA SEIPLE is the author of *Ghosts in the Fog: The Untold Story of Alaska's World War II Invasion* and *Byrd & Igloo: A Polar Adventure*. She has worked as a competitive intelligence specialist for a Fortune 500 company, as a librarian, and as a production editor and copy editor. Her education includes degrees in English, journalism, and library and information science. She lives in Asheville, North Carolina.